CROSSHAIRS

JACK CROSS SIG
BOOK 2

JACK DILLON

ROUGH
EDGES
PRESS

Crosshairs
Paperback Edition
Copyright © 2023 (As Revised) Jack Dillon

Rough Edges Press
An Imprint of Wolfpack Publishing
9850 S. Maryland Parkway, Suite A-5 #323
Las Vegas, Nevada 89183

roughedgespress.com

This book is a work of fiction. Any references to historical events, real people or real places are used fictitiously. Other names, characters, places and events are products of the author's imagination, and any resemblance to actual events, places or persons, living or dead, is entirely coincidental.

All rights reserved. No part of this book may be reproduced by any means without the prior written consent of the publisher, other than brief quotes for reviews.

Paperback ISBN 978-1-68549-279-3
eBook ISBN 978-1-68549-278-6

CROSSHAIRS

As far as she was aware, her husband worked for the Ministry of Defence, and that was as far as her knowledge went.

He looked at his wife and then glanced at Lizzie, who was oblivious to it all. She had learned a long time ago to tune out of their conversations; it was none of her business anyway.

Martha was referring to the attacks on the London underground on the seventh of July that year. It had followed the attack in New York almost four years previously when the war on terror had begun in earnest. This present attack had forced the government to take action by forming a tactical intelligence unit that targeted terrorism in all its guises and took the fight to them.

Bainbridge had just been given command of this new unit, and tonight's meal was to celebrate his promotion. All Martha knew, though, was that her husband had been promoted to a higher position within the Ministry of Defence and that it had something to do with recent events. Her husband never divulged any details about his work to her, which at times put a strain on their marriage.

He glanced out the window once more as the car stopped.

"We're here," he said.

As he got out and stood on the pavement, ready to help his wife out of the spacious interior, he said, "I've asked Tony to join us."

Just then, as all three of them were huddled together, four motorbikes skidded to a halt nearby, two at the rear of the car and the other two in front.

All four riders wore black, even down to helmets.

PROLOGUE I

JULY 2005—LONDON

General Bainbridge sat in the rear of the Bentley across from his wife and daughter.

They were all dressed for the evening's celebration: he was in a grey dinner suit by Tom Ford, his wife, Martha, in an elegant black Armani dress, and their twelve-year-old daughter, Elizabeth, also wore an Armani dress, but hers was white.

"Should we be celebrating tonight, dear? I mean, you know, after what has happened?" Martha asked, her eyes troubled.

"We might as well, dear. Who knows when we might get another chance. Besides, promotions like these are few and far between. I've worked hard for this opportunity, and I don't see why we can't enjoy the moment," Bainbridge replied, looking out the window.

"You know why, all those people..." she said, allowing her words to trail off. She never spoke of his work in front of Lizzie, not that she knew much about it anyway.

Bainbridge immediately sensed danger and shouted, "Get back in the car."

He pushed the two women into the Bentley once more as his driver, James Nicholson, a member of his security detail, came round to stand with him.

"Here, sir, my back-up piece," Nicholson said, thrusting a Walther PPS into his hand. "Now get back in the car with your family. I've called for back-up," he added, pushing Bainbridge back against the car.

Just as Bainbridge was debating whether or not to agree, gunfire raked the opposite side of the Bentley.

Bainbridge turned to see the two gunmen who had pulled up in front of the vehicle, firing at the car, hoping to kill the passengers inside.

Bystanders on the pavement outside the restaurant scattered in a wail of panicked screams, which galvanized Bainbridge into action. He aimed the Walther over the top of the car and fired.

His first shot glanced off the helmet of the gunman, knocking him off balance as the force pushed his head backward. Bainbridge's second shot hit him high on the chest, dropping him to the floor.

Nicholson had similar luck with the other gunman, dropping him with his first shot. Before he could acquire another target, a bullet hit him on his shoulder, spinning him around.

Bainbridge saw his driver take the hit and knew the shot had come from the two riders at the back of the car. Now they had clear targets.

He was standing on the pavement facing the front of the car, his left side leaning on the door. He saw Nicholson go down in front of him, then, to his left, over the top of the car, he saw one of the riders reach for the door handle to the rear seats.

He was divided in what to do. He knew the fourth rider was behind him, probably lining up a shot, but there was also this rider getting ready to open the door to reach his wife and daughter. For him, the choice was simple. He brought his Walther up over the top of the car just as he saw the man wrench open the passenger side door.

He heard a gunshot and felt something incredibly hard punch him high in his back. As he was half-turned, the impact felt as if it had struck him just above his left shoulder blade.

He was sent sprawling down the side of the car to land ungainly on the pavement not far from Nicholson.

He lay there, momentarily confused as to how he had ended up on the floor. He glanced to his right and saw Nicholson try to get up but was shot once more. This time the bullet hit him between his eyes, painting the ground with his blood and brain matter in a lurid Rorschach pattern.

Bainbridge managed to turn just in time to see the gunman walking over to him, gun extended, ready to fire.

Keeping his Walther low to the ground, he fired three shots at the man, hoping to hit a foot or ankle. The last bullet struck the man's right calf tearing through the muscle. He fell down, and Bainbridge shot him in the face, killing him instantly.

He lay back down, breathing heavily as the pain began to resonate through him, and then he heard several gunshots from inside the car.

Martha and Lizzie, he had to get to them.

Colonel Tony Armstrong had left the taxi further up the street. Something was happening and traffic had come to a standstill.

As he got out, he heard gunshots echoing through the night coming from the direction of the restaurant and he immediately feared the worst.

Being a member of the Security Services, he was required to be armed at all times. He took out a Walther PPS and jacked the slide on the run as he forced himself through the crowds. He just hoped he reached Bainbridge before it was too late.

Bainbridge dragged himself across the ground. He didn't know what he was going to do, just that he had to do something.

In his heart, he knew it was too late and that his wife and daughter were dead, but he was determined to get to their killer and make him pay.

He dragged himself level with the rear door. He reached up to grab the handle and dragged himself up. With all his rapidly waning strength, he pulled the door open and saw them.

His wife and daughter were lying on the seats, blood splashed all over them with a bullet hole in each of their foreheads.

The shock of seeing them like that was almost too much to bear. He screamed in anger and loss, and tears filled his eyes so that he was unable to see.

Suddenly he felt a gun barrel placed against the back of his head. He knew what it was, he actually longed for the trigger to be pulled so that he could be with his family. When he heard the shot so loud due to its close proximity, he was both angry and disappointed that he was still alive.

"General, are you hurt?" he heard Tony say when the echo of the gunshot had faded.

———

Tony arrived on the run. The crowds had dissipated by the time he reached the restaurant; the gunfire had scared them all into hiding, which was understandable.

The scene that greeted him was one of chaos and destruction. There were four bikes on the road, dead bodies on the ground, and he saw what appeared to be a biker standing over another figure with a gun to their head.

There was no time to ask questions, he had to act.

He brought up his Walther and fired.

———

Bainbridge turned and saw Tony standing there. He could only look at him; the words would not come.

Tony glanced over Bainbridge to see inside the car and immediately understood the man's distress. He placed a hand on Bainbridge's shoulder to comfort him, for he knew there were no words that would take this pain away.

PROLOGUE II

PRESENT DAY—SOMEWHERE IN SWITZERLAND

The man entered the room and looked at the large table before him.

Seated around it were faces he recognized, these were the players in the big game. All but one, the person seated at the head of the table, was shrouded in shadows. All he could make out was the shape of what appeared to be a man. These were the game changers. This was the High Council, only heard of in rumors and then only in whispers. The figure at the head of the table was known only to a few and by everyone else as Number One.

The men and women seated around this table held enough power to change the course of history. This was the Hierarchy.

"You have been summoned here because of the consequences we now face due to certain recent actions. Of late, those actions have brought this organization under some unwanted scrutiny from the security services of the United Kingdom. Granted, they are not the power they used to be, but they do have ties to the United States, and attention from that quarter would be both messy and, like everything that country does, a spectacular overreaction. So you are here to reverse that," the shadowy figure said.

This was an opportunity for him to cement his position within HATE, the Hierarchy for Anarchy, Terrorism, and Extortion—and ultimately, a seat at this table.

He felt his pulse quicken as he heard those words. They needed him.

"What do you have in mind?" he asked, keeping his voice calm and measured.

"You will finish what we started in 2005, you will destroy Special Intelligence Section Six."

CHAPTER ONE

Jack Cross looked down at the graves, his heart as heavy then as when his wife and daughter were first placed in them.

He knew he was torturing himself by visiting them, but what else could he do? He felt that to not visit them would be a betrayal of sorts.

He had told them both on numerous occasions when they had been alive of his love for them and that he would never, could never forget them. To stop visiting them would make a lie of all that.

It was a part of the grieving process, he was well aware of that, but it didn't help any. He was still too consumed by anger about their deaths to reconcile anything about his life and move on.

They had been brutally and callously murdered in front of him on his return from his last mission with SI6, a mission he was not even supposed to be on. He had agreed to help out his friend and partner, Mike Flynn, during which his friend had been injured in a helicopter crash and barely escaped with his life. On his return home, a hitman sent by the Hierarchy forced his way into their home and incapacitated Jack before shooting his wife and daughter in front of him. It was an act of cruelty designed to break his spirit, but unfortunately for the hit man, it had the opposite effect. Jack had survived, the hit man had not.

Now he faced a life without his family, without a future. Instead of love, his life was filled with hatred and anger toward those who had done this to him. All he could contemplate was revenge.

If his wife had still been alive, she would have pointed out the futility of his feelings. She had always been his anchor to the real world. Whenever he went on a mission, knowing she was waiting at home for his return was what made him strive to stay alive, to not take risks for risk's sake alone. Without her and his daughter, he had lost that anchor. He had nothing to keep him grounded. He no longer cared if he lived or died, just as long as he ensured those responsible died first.

He could see no way forward other than to take the fight to the Hierarchy; he would have to go back to work.

With one last look at his wife's grave, he said, "Forgive me," then turned around and walked out of the graveyard.

Special Intelligence Section Six Headquarters was situated in an abandoned underground railway tunnel deep in the bowels of London.

Commander Jonathan Dark walked through the corridor leading to the inner sanctum where General Donald Bainbridge ruled. His long legs ate up the ground with every stride. His flashing hazel eyes took in his surroundings, noting every detail as this was the first time he had been here. He'd worked for SI6 on a number of jobs, but that was as backup for the agents on the ground.

When he reached Bainbridge's outer office, he was met by Jennifer Austin, and a smile crossed his rugged face as he saw her for the first time.

Jennifer Austin was twenty-eight yet looked easily a decade younger. She had long blonde hair tied back in a ponytail that hung down her slender back and ice-blue eyes that hinted at mischievousness. Her sensuous full lips parted as if to say something as she noticed his intense stare.

"You must be Commander Dark," she said, not put off by the attention. It was something she had got used to and used many times to her advantage in her previous career in Military Intelligence before being asked by Bainbridge to work at her present post.

Clearing his throat, John said, "Correct, and you are?"

"Pleased to meet you, Commander. Go right in, the General is expecting you," she replied as her eyes admired his six foot three, broad-shouldered frame.

He noticed the smirk flash across her full lips, and then she was all business once more.

"Thanks," he said, and moved to the thick oak door. He admired her without knowing anything about her; she was the type of confident woman that met the world on her own terms and that you had to respect. There was much more to this woman than seen on that first quick glance, and he wondered if he would ever get to learn more.

He opened the door and entered the inner sanctum of the organization he'd only known about from whispers for years. He'd even worked for them, but still, their reputation was something of an urban legend in the intelligence community. No one really knew the true workings of SI6. His invite here today may be their way of opening up to him at least.

The room before him was brightly lit, had rich carpeting on the floor, softening the sound of his footsteps as he walked across it. A large mahogany desk sat at the far end, behind which sat a large man with a military bearing and a barrel chest.

Against the wall on his right stood a bookcase, and a single landscape by Turner hung on the wall behind the desk. To his left was a large Adam fireplace with a pile of wood stacked at the side, ready to be used.

"Come in, Commander, take a seat," Bainbridge said as he looked up from his work, greeting the Commander with a smile.

"Thank you, sir," John said, accepting the seat. He waited for Bainbridge to start the briefing, for that was what he assumed he was there for.

"You're looking fit and well, John, good," Bainbridge said as his eyes met the man before him.

"Thank you, sir, I am," John replied.

"Okay, down to business. The last time you helped us out was up in Scotland back in July. You saw what happened, but you may not be aware of what happened upon our return," Bainbridge said.

"If you're referring to Jack Cross' family being killed in that accident, I am, sir."

"Ah yes, the car crash," Bainbridge muttered, remembering the official report he had put out over the incident, which covered up the real details.

John's eyes narrowed as he asked, "Are you saying the report was falsified, sir?"

"That's exactly what I'm saying, but it's not what you

think. A member of the group we were fighting in Scotland attacked Jack Cross in his own home. They sent a hitman to terminate him. He killed Cross' pregnant wife and daughter in front of him before Jack got the better of him. To spare him undue attention from the media and to rob the group who originated the hit of their glory, I issued a more sanitized version of events for the report."

"I see, sir."

"That, in part, is why I have summoned you here. To give Jack Cross time to grieve over his loss and because Mike Flynn, our only other operative, is recuperating from his injuries, our ranks are seriously depleted. I have spoken with your superiors in the Special Boat Squadron, and they have agreed to a secondment on a temporary basis at first. I'm sure I can always find work for a man of your abilities in this organization, but that decision will be left up to you. As you are aware, you will be working under and bound by the Official Secrets Act, something that you are used to already, I'm sure. The benefits of working here, among others, are an increase in pay, obviously. This will be on a temporary footing until you either return to your unit or become a full-time employee. Any thoughts, Commander?"

John sat back, looking at the General. For the last four years, he had led 'C' Squadron of the SBS, something he was extremely proud of and enjoyed immensely. Could he leave that behind and work for Bainbridge? He would still get to travel, would still get to protect his country using the skills he'd learned in the Navy. He would still have all the excitement that came with the job: being able to drive around in fast vehicles, use firearms, blow shit up, all the things he loved about his work, but he would have to leave all his mates behind. This job had helped him be the best person he could possibly be, and along the way, he'd made some fantastic friends.

"What exactly will my duties be, sir?" he asked, stalling whilst his mind mulled over the problem, turning the decision over in his mind.

"You will be an agent, or operative, for this organization. As you already know, we fight against terrorism in all its forms. What you may not be aware of, is that we take the fight to them. We do not wait around for legislation to act on this country's behalf; we act swiftly and decisively. Some of what you will be tasked to do may be described as the work of an assassin, but I would rather consider it the work of a skilled surgeon. Killing someone, whatever the reason behind it, is never easy and should never be so. If I thought you found it easy, you would not be here. You are a skilled soldier though, and killing is part of your job description, however you may like to call it, so it's not something that would be new to you. Does that answer your question? And remember, before you decide, you are bound by the Official Secrets Act."

He was aware this was an opportunity that didn't come around too often, so he sat up straight and said, "I'm in."

"Welcome, Commander, to SI6."

CHAPTER TWO

The plane had landed at Heathrow airport from Geneva and taxied to the terminal. He had debarked with all the other passengers.

It had been decided to arrive unannounced on a commercial flight rather than on a private plane. He was under strict orders by the Hierarchy to keep a low profile until he was ready to make his move. At that time, they had given him carte blanche to do whatever he thought necessary to bring down SI6.

He had some ideas, but it would take some planning, and acquiring the right personnel was crucial to that.

Taking on a military tactical intelligence unit would not be easy. Destroying them would be even harder. What the Hierarchy had tasked him with seemed, at face value, to be an impossible mission. It was a challenge, he had no doubt about that, but impossible, he hardly thought so. Very few things in this world were truly impossible if you had the intellect and the drive to face the challenge. Those two things he had in abundance, so the rest would just be down to planning.

There was a black Bentley waiting for him as he left the 'Arrivals' terminal and he climbed aboard.

"Take me to my hotel," he commanded before closing the panel between him and the driver.

He had been chosen for this task not just because he was the best man for the job. He had worked for the Hierarchy for as long as he could remember; while his brother was working his way up through the ranks of the Mafia, he was building a name and reputation within HATE. After a career in the Spetsnaz, he resigned his commission to enter the private sector and was quickly scooped up by HATE. When his brother had been killed in a boating accident just off the coast of Crete earlier this year, he had been recalled from a camp in Afghanistan, where he had been training terrorist recruits for various organizations funded by the Hierarchy. It had been called an accident by the media that had reported the incident, but he had been given the true facts by one of the groups that had investigated it for the Hierarchy. The investigation had turned up traces of C4 used to blow up the yacht his brother had been on.

He would have taken this operation on whether his brother had been involved or not, but because of his sibling's involvement, he would've done this for free.

Andrei Petrov took out his phone and dialed a number. When it was answered, he said, "I'm on my way to the hotel, assemble the men."

"What's the op?" asked the voice on the other end.

"We are here to close down an account," he said, not using plain language being conscious of being overheard.

"Is this official or personal?" asked the voice.

"Not that it's any of your concern, but both," he replied angrily. He didn't feel he should have to explain himself to a subordinate, something he would rectify at the earliest convenience.

"Good, if it's official, we are guaranteed payment, not so much if it's personal," replied the voice, making a point he couldn't really argue with, but it still rankled with him that it had to be voiced.

Andrei calmed himself, then said, "Operation Orion begins in twelve hours, so tell the men they had better be ready," and he ended the call before the voice could argue further.

———

Mike Flynn looked out of the window of his hospital room.

All he could see were the grounds of the hospital. There was a tree-lined green right in front of his room with a few benches for the patients to sit on should the weather allow it. As the season was changing, that opportunity became less frequent.

He hadn't been allowed out there just yet, there was some concern about his recovery. It wasn't going as expected.

When he was in the helicopter that crashed in the Loch back in July, he was lucky he hadn't died. If it hadn't been for the intervention of his friend, Jack Cross, he most certainly would have. He came away from there with several broken bones and other injuries. It was these other injuries that had the doctors worried. His spleen and one of his kidneys were bruised, which called for a longer recuperation period. His right knee had sustained quite a bit of damage too, requiring some surgical restructuring. At the moment, he was wearing a caliper to aid with his mobility, but the doctors were concerned that if the repair didn't hold, he would need a completely new joint. If that happened, he would be out of action for a lot longer than they had first thought.

All this sitting around was not doing him much good. He longed to be back out in the field working, but he needed to be signed off first. He had to admit though, he didn't feel at his best. Perhaps a few more weeks wouldn't hurt. He wondered how Jack was doing.

Once he came around from the first batch of surgery, Tony informed him of what went down at the Cross household.

It was a tragedy, and he knew exactly what his friend was going through. He knew him probably better than anyone on the planet. Jack would be blaming himself for what had happened, and he would most definitely be contemplating revenge.

If he wasn't stopped, there would be a trail of dead bodies strewn all around London.

CHAPTER THREE

Colonel Anthony (Tony) Armstrong put away his phone. He had just called the private hospital where Mike Flynn was being treated to check on his status. He did it every day just to keep abreast of how he was doing.

He knew well enough how easy it was for operatives to start feeling depressed when they were inactive for whatever reasons. Mike's were valid reasons, his injuries made him unfit for duty.

Tony's vigilance was twofold: firstly, and what he would like to think was most important, was Mike was a friend. Secondly, which Bainbridge knew was the most important, he was an asset to the organization, and he had to keep up to date on his progress. If it turned out his injuries precluded him from active service, then he was no longer of any use to them, and steps would have to be taken.

He was not happy with what the doctors were telling him about Mike's progress. He didn't seem to be recovering fast enough, and there were a few complications they had not foreseen.

They needed Mike back up and running once more. With Jack Cross on indefinite leave while he grieved over the loss of his family, they were severely hampered by the lack of adequate operatives. Bainbridge had a plan to recruit Commander Dark of the Special Boat Service. He would be a good replacement, but they would still be severely undermanned if he agreed. He dreaded passing on the details of this information to his boss.

"How is he?" a voice behind him asked. He turned to see General Donald Bainbridge standing there with a rare look of concern etched on his face.

"He's getting better, but it's going to take more time. He may never be one hundred percent again, you realize that, don't you?" Tony replied.

"Yes, Tony, I'm well aware of that possibility as dire as that may be, but, as always, the show must go on."

"You've spoken to Commander Dark?"

"Yes, and he's agreed to come aboard, for the time being at least."

"Well, that should help should we get a case dropped on us."

"Have you spoken to Jack recently?"

"No, sir, I thought it best to give him some time alone to get through this."

"Let's hope he does it soon and comes back to work."

"With respect, sir, what he's going through now is a direct result of him working for us. I think it safe to say I won't be holding my breath for him to come back any time soon."

Bainbridge looked at Tony; he knew things looked bad at the moment for his organization. He was not about to allow this to finish what he'd been working so hard to keep moving forward for the past fifteen years though. He came to a decision.

Nodding his head, he said, "Perhaps you're right. Maybe it's time we did what we should have done a long time ago. It's time we went on a recruiting drive."

Andrei picked up the bottle and looked at the label. Stolichnaya Elit, one of the very best vodkas in the world. He poured himself a shot glass full and then tossed it back. He closed his eyes as he felt the liquor hit his stomach.

He glanced at his watch. Just two hours to go before Operation Orion began and he would target SI6.

He opened his laptop and connected to the Internet. From his jacket pocket, he took a flash drive he'd been given after his meeting with the High Council. They said it contained all the information he needed to complete his mission.

Looking at it in the palm of his hand, he said softly, "Okay, let's see what you have."

He plugged the drive into the USB port in the side of his laptop, clicked the link that came up, and instantly, a new screen appeared. On it was a list of names, each with a link to a file. He clicked on the first link, and the file opened up, revealing all the details pertaining to the name it belonged to.

"Interesting," he said as he quickly read through the file. "How on earth did you get a hold of all this? It's clearly highly classified material." he wondered as he stepped back.

He glanced through the window. London stretched out below, and lights were coming on all over the city as night drew in around it like a warm blanket.

He poured himself another shot of vodka and held it up to the window.

"To Grigori, I'll make them pay, little brother, blood for blood," he toasted, then tossed down the drink.

As he turned back to his laptop to read the rest of the files, three huge explosions lit up the darkening sky around the city.

Keeping his attention on the laptop, he said, "And so it begins."

CHAPTER FOUR

"Turn on the news," Tony said, bursting into Bainbridge's office.

When Bainbridge looked up and saw the look in his Chief of Staff's eyes, he knew it was bad.

He turned to the wall behind him; beneath the landscape by Turner that hung, there was a panel, barely visible. He touched a section of the wall, and the panel slid across, revealing a screen. Picking up a remote from inside a drawer in his desk, he turned on the screen. He quickly found the BBC News Channel and his eyes went wide when he saw what was being reported.

"When did this happen?" he asked, his voice raw with emotion.

"The explosions all went off within the last half hour. All three detonations were timed to go off simultaneously, sir. This was a planned event," Tony replied as he stared at the devastation displayed on the screen.

"Has anyone come forward to take credit for the act yet?" Bainbridge asked as he stared at the screen also.

"Not yet, the police are handling it so far, and their

anti-terrorist units will be taking point, I would have thought."

"Quite," Bainbridge commented almost absent-mindedly. He could not tear his eyes away from the scenes of horror being displayed by the news channel.

"Do you think this has anything to do with us? Could it be the Hierarchy, do you think?" Tony asked.

"For what purpose?"

"For revenge, of course, we did stop their attempt to get the NOC list not so long ago. If they are as far-reaching as we were led to believe, then it's safe to assume they would not allow this to pass without some sort of payback."

"That thought occurred to me too," Bainbridge agreed. He reached for the intercom and said, "Miss Austin, get hold of Commander Dark and tell him to report in immediately."

"Right away, sir," Jen replied.

"If it is the Hierarchy, we can expect more...a lot more," Tony said.

Bainbridge looked at Tony and his face darkened. "You'd better get in touch with Jack and inform him he may have a target on his back. Also, increase security at the hospital where Mike is staying. We can't take any chances there either."

"If the Hierarchy do have Jack in their crosshairs, he is the last man they should mess with right now," Tony said.

"Agreed, but inform him anyway."

"I'm on it, sir," Tony said, taking out his phone as he turned to leave the room.

———

John was in the armory with Major Arthur Bacon, a thirty-year veteran who had been seconded from the SAS to work with SI6. Close to retirement, his hair was almost all white, and there was an air of restlessness about him. His wiry five-feet-ten frame was always on the move. It was his expertise with weapons that had brought him to his present post, and it was his duty to ensure the operatives were always geared up with the best available.

"Welcome to the Basement, Commander," Bacon said as John walked through the door.

"Major Bacon, I heard you were dead," joked John.

"I may as well be. I've been buried down here for as long as I can remember," Bacon replied.

"I must say it's a pleasure, sir, you're a legend," John said, thrusting his hand out to shake the Major's. The formalities over with, John said, "General Bainbridge has ordered me down here to get re-equipped."

"Okay then, let's see what you've been using," Bacon said, stepping back to see what he had.

John took out his pistol, a Sig Saur 230, and laid it in the Major's hand.

"Not a bad weapon, good for concealed carry, but the stopping power could be better. Let me see what we have here," he said, turning to a rack of pistols up against the wall. "What's your preference, Commander? Do you have one?" he asked.

"I'll leave it up to you, sir, you're the expert. I'm just a simple soldier."

"Well, I doubt that very much, or you wouldn't be here, and we wouldn't be having this conversation. Here try this," Bacon said, reaching for one of the pistols.

John looked at the pistol, a Sig P250.

"Nice," John said as he checked it out.

"It's chambered for the 9x19. The magazine holds fifteen rounds plus one in the breach. Try it out," Bacon told him.

John looked around and saw the firing range. Bacon handed him a full mag, and the two of them walked over to the range. He checked to see the gun was safe, that no rounds had been left inside, and the safety was in the 'on' position, all standard operating procedures when handling weapons of any kind. He pushed the mag into the butt, then jacked the slide to inject a round into the breach. He picked up a pair of ear defenders and placed them over his head. Bacon did likewise.

Flipping the safety off, he assumed the stance and readied himself.

He fired off three rounds in rapid succession to test the feel, the recoil, and the aim. His next three were accurate as he compensated for the action. His final three shots finished off his session.

"I'm done. I'll take one, please. Can I have it gift-wrapped?" John asked, keeping a straight face.

Bacon brought the target up the range to inspect. The first three shots were center mass in an area of around six inches in diameter. The next three were tightly grouped over the heart, and the last three were dead center in the forehead, right above the eye line.

"I'm impressed, Commander. There's nothing I can do for you now, is there?" Bacon asked.

John's phone rang and he answered it, "Yes?"

"The General wants you in his office now, there's been an incident," Jen said.

"I'm on my way," he replied and put his phone away.

"Duty calls, sir," he told the Major and quickly walked towards the door. He grabbed three extra mags on his way out and a holster for the Sig and was gone.

CHAPTER FIVE

Jack Cross was sitting in his kitchen at home, a steaming cup of tea on the table in front of him.

All signs of the mayhem that took place in that house a few weeks earlier had been scrubbed clean, so only his memories remained.

On the table next to his cup was his phone, which started to ring. He saw the caller ID and picked it up.

"Hi, Tony, I wondered when you'd get round to calling," he said.

"Jack, there's been an incident, you need to come in. I can't discuss it over an unsecured line, but be aware you could be at risk if you remain at large."

"An incident? What's happened?"

"Turn on the news, it's all over it, then get your arse in here. Jack, I'm not asking, I'm telling you," Tony replied.

Jack turned off his phone and then reached for the remote to turn on the small fourteen-inch TV on the kitchen worktop. He never wanted it in there, but

Melissa had said it would help their daughter eat her meals better.

The screen came alive and he changed the channel to the news. Reports were still covering the trio of explosions that had rocked the city earlier.

He watched for a few moments, learning the salient facts about the incident, then turned off the TV.

He went up the stairs to his bedroom, where he took out his footlocker from beneath the bed. He opened it and reached inside to take out his pistol. He still had the Walther CCP (Concealed Carry Pistol) from the last mission for SI6, along with the holster. He put the holster on, placed the Walther inside, then shrugged into a casual jacket.

As he walked down the stairs towards the front door, he actually felt his spirits rise a little. This was what he needed, something to take his mind off his present situation, something to vent his fury on. If the Hierarchy were involved in this, then that would be even better. He was wondering how he could take the fight to them, and then this happened.

A smile crossed his face as he opened the door.

Karma was an unsympathetic wheel, but this time, it seemed to be turning favorably in his direction for a change.

Andrei watched the news being reported on the TV with a satisfied smile on his face. Everything was going according to plan so far.

He had teams mixing with the bystanders who would gravitate to the disaster areas just to rubberneck; they would be indistinguishable from everyone else. London was truly a cosmopolitan city, and his team would just be more faces in a sea of faces.

They would be there, though, when their targets arrived to investigate, and then the games would truly begin.

Until then, he would just sit back and wait for the fun to start.

By the time Jack reached SI6 HQ, things were moving along.

He walked through the corridor to Bainbridge's office and saw Jen leaving her office.

"Ah, Jack, I was told you were coming in. You're to go down to R&D. Tony and Commander Dark are already down there," she said, cutting him off.

He was glad she didn't ask how he was; he was fed up of hearing that question. Honestly, he didn't know how he was, just that he had to do something, and this, what he was doing now, was that something.

"I understand, from the news reports, that all hell's broken loose," he said.

"You could say that. I haven't seen this much panic from the security services since 9/11," she replied.

"It's bad then," he agreed.

"You know the way, they're waiting for you," she said as she headed off in another direction.

If things were as bad as they were back when 9/11 happened, then this was surely as bad as it gets. If the Hierarchy were involved, then SI6 should take point on this. They knew more about the shadowy group than anyone on the planet.

Then it struck him.

That's what Tony meant when he'd said he was in danger. This was somehow related to an attack on SI6 for what they did recently by scuppering their plans to acquire a NOC list.

He quickened his pace.

When he entered R&D, he immediately saw Tony standing with Commander Dark and Robert Deakin, the remarkable man in charge. A small man with a large intellect, he'd run R&D for some years.

He saw Deakin turn as he entered.

"It's getting rather crowded in here," Deakin said as he pushed his horn-rimmed glasses up the bridge of his nose. He liked it best when he was left alone down in the lower levels with just his meager staff and his computers.

"Ah, Jack, glad you could make it here," Tony said when he, too, turned to see what Deakin had meant.

"You left me little choice, Colonel," Jack said. He walked over to them nodding a greeting to the Commander. The last time he'd seen Dark was in Scotland when they had finished off the Hierarchy's attempt at distributing the NOC list to anyone willing to pay the right price.

"We're just checking out CCTV cameras covering the sites of the recent explosions to see if anyone pops up via our facial recognition software," Tony explained.

"What have you turned up?" Jack asked.

"Nothing yet, but it's early days," John told him as Tony returned his attention to the bank of monitors they were scanning.

"Shouldn't we be out there investigating?" Jack asked.

"Yes, good idea. Go, all of you, and leave me to my work. I'll inform you the moment I have anything," Deakin blurted out before Tony could say anything.

Clearly, the technician was eager to get them out of his already thinning hair.

Tony looked down at the smaller man, who seemed to wilt beneath his withering stare.

"Okay, Deakin, you win. But contact me the second you have anything," he chided.

"I will, now go, please," urged the little man.

Jack saw Deakin breathe a sigh of relief the moment Tony moved away. He'd forgotten how intimidated he always was by the Colonel, it made him smile.

As they left R&D, Tony said, "Here's the plan then. Three of us, three blast sites; we each take one and report on our findings. Are we clear on that?"

Nods from the other two told the colonel they understood.

"Keep your earbuds in and turned on at all times, and keep your eyes open for possible threats. We don't know what we're facing here as of yet, so no taking chances, is that clear, Jack?" Tony said.

"Why're you targeting me with that comment?" Jack asked.

"You know why," Tony said, and he fixed him with a knowing stare.

"You have no need to worry on my account, I'll do my job," Jack told him.

"Right then, let's go," Tony said and led the way to the elevator.

CHAPTER SIX

Jack reached the site of the explosion.

There was a massive police presence, as was to be expected, and the entire area was cordoned off.

Nothing new there.

What was new was the fact that all three explosions were co-ordinated to detonate simultaneously. That took a lot of organizing and expertise to pull off. The timing had to be spot on, which also showed they had plenty of time to plan it.

He was connected via his ear bud to the HQ network and he said, "I don't like this."

"What don't you like, Jack?" asked Bainbridge.

He was monitoring the three investigations from the Situation Room along with Deakin from R&D. In front of the two of them was a bank of monitors relaying all the data from the three operatives in a live stream.

"Everything smacks of this operation being well planned; the timing to get all three bombs to go off at the same time takes phenomenal planning. This though, there's something wrong about all this," Jack said as he stood outside the cordon looking in at the scene.

"Explain, Jack, what are you seeing?" Bainbridge asked, his voice taut with tension.

"Well, first off, it's a minor subway station,. Yes, there's going to be disruption but not the same as if they had hit Piccadilly or somewhere like that. It's almost like they tried to keep the casualties to a minimum but at the same time make as big a statement as possible."

"What else?" asked Bainbridge, who could tell Jack wasn't finished.

Jack scanned the crowd of bystanders; it was the usual bunch of rubberneckers all staring at the scene, getting some sort of macabre enjoyment from it all. Slowly he looked at every face, nothing seemed out of the ordinary at first, but then, there it was.

One person was looking in the wrong direction. Instead of staring at the scene beyond the cordon, this one person was staring straight at him.

He tried to hide it, of course. The moment their eyes met, he looked away, but it was too late. Jack had seen him, and he knew he had something to do with it all.

Jack moved away from the cordon, and keeping his eyes firmly on his target, he moved towards him.

"I have a target, they may have been involved," he said.

"Describe them and we'll get them under surveillance," Bainbridge said.

Jack forced his way through the crowds, but it was slow going, and although he knew he'd been, made he didn't want to draw any undue attention to himself. Tread carefully was the name of the game.

"He's wearing jeans and a red hoody pulled over his head so I can't get a good look at his face. He's around six feet tall, average build, and he's made me, I'm sure of it," Jack said as he moved towards him.

"Are you sure?" Bainbridge asked.

"I'm positive, he's moving off, I'm in pursuit," Jack told him. He heard another voice in his ear.

"I have him, sir," Deakin told Bainbridge. He was watching the whole thing too, all three incidents on three separate monitors. Jack was the first on the scene, and having widened the scope, he had now picked up the red hoody leaving with Jack in pursuit.

Jack could see quite clearly the red hoody bobbing and weaving through the crowd. He kept him in sight as the two of them moved further away from the subway station.

As the crowd thinned, Jack wondered where he was going, where was he taking him?

A couple were blocking his path as he followed red hoody along the pavement. As he tried to maneuver around them, they seemed to stutter as they blocked his path in that little dance you do when both parties go the same way.

"Sorry," Jack apologized as he tried to get around them as they collided briefly. During the collision, he felt a sharp nip on his arm, nothing more than a scratch really, and because his attention was focused on red hoody, he didn't give it another thought as he got around the couple. With a wave and another apology he was past them and he saw red hoody dive around a corner.

"He's making his move," he said and gave chase.

By the time he reached the corner and looked down the street, there was no sign of him.

"He's gone," he said angrily, "I've lost him."

CHAPTER SEVEN

Tony reached the site of the second explosion seconds after the news of Jack losing red hoody was sinking in at HQ.

"Tony keep your eyes open for anyone looking out for you," Bainbridge said.

Tony immediately went on alert.

"What's happened?" he asked as he looked around the area. It was similar to the one Jack had just left; a substation surrounded by a crowd of macabre watchers. The surrounding area had been cordoned off by the police, and there was an armed police presence evident.

Tony looked all around him, and just like at the previous scene, all eyes were on what was happening at the station, all except one.

"Jack saw someone at the other site who was watching for one of us and not what was going on. The moment he arrived, this person left. Jack gave chase but lost him in the crowd," Bainbridge explained.

"Okay, well, I have one here too. There could be a pattern forming here," Tony said.

"What's going on, Tony?" Bainbridge asked; Tony heard a little concern in his voice.

"The usual stuff, armed police protecting the scene while investigators do their thing, then there's this guy."

"What's he look like so we can get him on CCTV?" Bainbridge asked.

"He's wearing jeans and a red hoody."

"You're serious?"

"Red hoody, you say? I've got one of those here right now," John said.

He was at the third explosion site. He'd arrived just as Tony was giving his report.

"What's going on? Can someone explain, please?" John asked.

Back at the second bombsite, Tony kept his eyes on red hoody.

"So there's been one of these red hoodies at each site?" he said.

"It's looking that way," Bainbridge affirmed.

"Got eyes on him now. What are your orders?" Tony asked.

"You have a new objective now, detain the red hoody," Bainbridge said quickly.

"Copy that," Tony said.

The entire time he was speaking with HQ, he had eyes on his target, and the moment he moved toward him, he saw him turn and look right at him.

"Whoa!" he said. "I've just been made," he added.

He saw the figure turn and quickly move away.

"He's on the move," Tony said as he made to follow.

"Do not lose him," Bainbridge ordered.

"I'm on it," Tony agreed.

He forged through the crowd, hoping to keep tabs on him. The throng closed in around him, making it difficult for him to move. They all wanted to see more of what was happening at the bombsite.

Over the sea of heads, he could just about keep the red hoody in sight.

Tony used his broad shoulders to force his way through a bunch of people blocking his path. He had to pass between two people who seemed intent on stopping him. He shouldered through them, and as he passed by the woman, her male companion pushed Tony.

"Sorry, mate," he said as Tony glowered at him. He felt a sudden scratch on his arm. He spun around to look at the culprit, but they had gone.

He continued his pursuit and saw red hoody turn a corner. When he reached the same spot though, there was no sign of him.

"Shit!" he exclaimed, "I lost him," he added as he slammed his hand against the wall, furious with himself.

"Come back to base, Tony," Bainbridge told him. "It's up to you now, Commander," he added.

"I have eyes on," John said. He'd spotted the red hoody and was moving to intercept.

Again, as with the other two, the crowd was thick, and he felt like a salmon swimming upstream as he fought his way through them.

He felt a sharp nick on the back of his arm as he

passed between a couple but thought nothing of it, as he was too intent on keeping red hoody in sight.

As the crowd thinned, he saw him duck around a corner, and he raced to keep up, but when he got there, he was gone.

"Oh fuck, I lost the fucker," he snarled.

He carried on walking to see if he could pick up a sight of him, and then he saw it.

In a waste bin on the edge of the pavement was stuffed a red hoody.

He took it out to examine it and he recognized it as the one worn by the man he chased.

"Er, guys, I think we have a problem," he said.

CHAPTER EIGHT

Jack was the first one back to HQ and he went straight to the Situation Room.

"What happened out there?" Bainbridge shouted.

Jack walked up to the man, stared him right in the eye, and said, "I lost him okay. It happens, shit happens, sir."

Bainbridge took a breath and said, "You're right, Jack. I wasn't blaming you. It seems all three of you faced the same thing. This was planned, quite professionally, I might add."

"You sound impressed," Jack accused.

"What they did, not in the slightest, how they did it, possibly. It took precise planning to pull this off, which shows that it took time and resources."

"Who do we know with those sort of resources?" Jack asked.

"Oh, any number of terrorist groups could have done this, what bothers me is why. What is their endgame?"

"Well, it seems they wanted us there, or they wouldn't have worn these," John said as he entered the Situation

Room. He was carrying the red hoody he found in the waste bin.

"Yep, the one I chased wore one just like that," Jack agreed.

"So did mine," Tony added as he entered the room.

"So what do we know then from all this?" Bainbridge asked as he looked at all of them.

"Three sites, three red hoodies, they expected us to show up, and they wanted us to see them," Jack observed.

"I agree, but why? What possible motive could they have?" Bainbridge asked.

Jack looked at the others. He saw John scratch his arm. He glanced at his own arm as a thought hit him. He quickly replayed the events of the chase through his mind before asking his next question.

"Did either of you collide with anyone, like a couple, for example?"

Both Tony and John looked at him. John voiced the frustration they were both feeling. "Are you serious? It was total chaos out there."

"Did you bump into a couple or have to get past someone then feel something dig into your arm, like a scratch or something? Something you'd quickly push to the back of your mind because you were focusing on the red hoody?" Jack asked again.

Tony looked at him and then at John, who wore the same expression as he did. They both knew he was right.

Jack saw it too. As quick as a flash, Deakin was at his side with a scanner in his hand.

"Where did you feel it?" Deakin asked.

Jack pointed to his arm and Deakin placed the small device over it and a beep was heard.

Deakin looked up at Bainbridge, his eyes wide.

"He's been implanted with a sub-dermal tracker," he said.

Tony and John looked at their arms and then at Bainbridge as the importance of what had happened sank in.

"This was planned from the start. The bombs were just to get us out there. Three teams of three, one distracts while the other two inject whichever one of us turned up. They knew we were severely handicapped and would only send one man to each site. It was all to get a tracker implanted in one of us," Bainbridge said, laying it all out for them.

"They know exactly where we are," Jack stated the obvious.

"Why though? They can't possibly plan on attacking us in here," Tony postulated.

"We don't even know who 'they' are as yet," John said. As he looked at the others, he added, "Or do we?"

Tony turned to Bainbridge and said, "The Hierarchy?"

"From what we learned about them, which is not much, we assume they have the potential to pull something of this magnitude off," agreed Bainbridge.

"You mean that outfit we faced in Scotland not too long ago?" John asked. When he saw them both agree, he said, "Well, I suppose they would want their revenge, we did put a dent in their operation."

"There's no proof it was them yet, but we cannot rule them out. We have made many enemies since we began operations, so until we're certain of who's behind this, we have to take precautions," Bainbridge said.

Jack asked, "What about this?" holding up his arm. "What are we going to do about this? Can you remove it?" he reminded them.

Deakin glanced at Bainbridge and then looked at him. "Without a thorough examination to see where it is and what it's made of, there's no way I can decide that," he confessed.

"That's just great. That means we can't go anywhere without them knowing our every move," Jack exploded.

"Is there any way to mask the signature of the tracker, or at the very least, determine its range?" Tony asked, hoping to calm the tension in the room down a notch.

"Do we even know if these things are trackers or not yet?" Tony asked.

Deakin looked at him and it was as if something had dawned on him. His eyes went wide, and his mouth gaped open.

"Shit! I never even considered anything else," he blurted out.

Adjusting the handheld device, he grabbed Jack's arm and placed the scanner over it once more.

Jack's color drained from his face as the possibility of something far worse than a tracker hit him.

Deakin passed the scanner over his arm where Jack had first indicated, then he breathed deeply, the obvious relief showing on his face. He relaxed his shoulders as he said, "It's okay, it's just a tracker."

"What am I missing here?" John asked when everyone seemed to have calmed down somewhat.

Tony turned to him to explain. "There are sub-dermal implants that are loaded with explosives, not a great deal as you can imagine due to their size, but just enough to rupture an artery or cause a hemorrhage, depending on where they're injected."

John gulped and turned to Deakin, "You're sure it's a tracker?" he asked, grabbing hold of the smaller man's arm.

"I'm sure, Commander, you are quite safe," Deakin informed him.

"Well, that's a relative term considering the game we're in, but way better than having a bomb inside me," John clarified.

Jack turned to Deakin to pose a question. "Is there any way you could track the signal coming from this, you know, reverse it and track the tracker, see where they are?"

"That's a very good idea," Deakin said as he walked over to the bank of computers nearby. He placed the scanner down on a desk and went to work on the keyboard, his fingers dancing lightly over the keys like a concert pianist playing a concerto.

"If I can recognize the signal wavelength the tracker is using, I may be able to track it back to its source. I should be able to turn the tables and, as Captain Cross suggested, track the tracker," Deakin muttered as he worked feverishly.

"How long will this take, Deakin?" Bainbridge asked impatiently.

"How long is a piece of string? I won't know until I've finished, sir. This is not an easy task," Deakin grumbled.

"We're on the clock here, Deakin. Time is not something we have in abundance," insisted Bainbridge.

"I am well aware of the constraints placed upon us, sir, but applying pressure where none can be applied is a useless task, I can assure you," argued Deakin.

Bainbridge was about to rebuke him, but a look from his Chief of Staff hinted at another course of action. Instead, he said, "Do your best."

"I have it," Deakin said, standing up to grin at them in satisfaction.

CHAPTER NINE

Andrei was feeling extremely pleased with himself. His plan was going wonderfully smoothly. He didn't like to think it, for it was such a cliché, but it was moving like a well-oiled machine.

Nine people were standing in front of him, six men and three women. One man stood in the center at the front, he was Viktor, and he led this team. These were the ones who had played such an important role in the game so far, for they had begun the game.

"I must congratulate you all on a job well done. It's not over yet though. As soon as we have word, the next phase will be put into play. Go prepare yourselves. You must be ready to move as soon as the word comes in," he ordered.

The nine figures moved out of his room, and Andrei turned to the small man sitting at the desk with a bank of three monitors arrayed before him. Other pieces of equipment were sitting behind the monitors and around the desk, most of which Andrei had no idea of their workings.

"How are we progressing, Sergei?" he asked.

The small man glanced up and smiled. "Any second now," he said.

Andrei nodded his head, "Good work," he said, taking out his phone and dialing. He held it to his ear and asked, "Boris, are you ready?"

"We are waiting for the word, that's all," replied the voice of his strike team leader.

"You have it then, execute," Andrei said, then put his phone away.

"I want security beefed up here. If you three walked in here with those trackers, then they know where this place is," Bainbridge commanded angrily.

"I'm on it," Tony said as he moved away, his phone already in his hand.

"I want all personnel armed at all times. I want perimeter guards with assault rifles. Every exit must have triple security, and I want it done now!" Bainbridge stormed.

He was furious that three of his operatives could have been compromised so easily. He turned to Jack, his eyes glaring at the tall man. "How in God's name could you allow them to tag you like that? I know you're still grieving over the loss of your family, but really, how could you be that stupid?" he railed.

"General, it was chaos out there," John interrupted.

Bainbridge turned to face the speaker, "Don't you dare interrupt me. If I was you, Commander, I'd shut the hell up. I'm coming to you in a moment, that goes for you too, Colonel," he snarled.

"All three of you have not only jeopardized this

mission but this Headquarters and everyone in this organization too."

Tony stepped forward. As Chief of Staff, he was the only one in the room who had clout enough to argue with their boss.

"With respect, sir, this could've happened to any operative. The fact that it happened to all three of us shows how professional and well-planned these people are," he said.

"That doesn't alter the fact that this was a complete debacle and we've been left totally vulnerable," Bainbridge countered.

"This will work out, sir," Tony said, sounding more convinced than he felt.

"It had better, Tony. It had better."

———

"Inspector Smith of the Metropolitan Protection Command, we're here to boost your security," the lead man in the nine-person team said at the entrance to the underground headquarters.

"Hold on, sir, while I verify," the guard said. He reached for a phone hung on the wall.

Smith placed a small device beneath the desk the guard was standing behind the instant he turned to reach for the phone.

After a quick call, the guard returned the handset to the cradle and said to the group, "Okay, sir, go right on in."

The six men and three women walked through the entrance and into the bowels of SI6.

———

Bainbridge took out his phone as it rang.

"Sir, the extra security has arrived from Protection Command," Jen said.

"Thank you, Miss Austen," he replied, then put the phone away. He looked at Tony and told him, "At least Protection Command is on the ball, the extra guards are here."

"Already, that was quick," Tony said, checking his watch. "That must be a record, I only put in the request ten minutes ago."

Bainbridge looked at him, then at the others.

Jack saw the looks pass between them and knew something was wrong. What Tony had said was true, for the guards to get here so quickly was beyond comprehension.

"What are you two thinking, that these security guards are somehow part of the plot?" he asked.

Bainbridge took out his phone once more and made a quick call. He said, "General Bainbridge of Special Intelligence Section Six, have you sent out reinforcements to boost security?"

"We've sent out people to the entire Security Services, sir. Standard procedure for a terrorist event of this magnitude," replied the voice on the other end of the call.

"Of course it is, thank you," Bainbridge replied. "It's SOP for an event of this magnitude, as I knew, but I had to check. They sent them out the moment the bombs went off and it was identified as a terrorist event," he said, his face softening with relief.

The tension in the room eased a little with the news. Jack, though, remained wary. Something didn't seem quite right somehow. He kept his concerns to himself, as he didn't want to alarm anyone in case what he felt was unfounded and a residue of his grief was somehow heightening all his concerns.

Instead, he simply watched.

Inspector Smith touched his ear bud and said, "Okay, we're in."

"Proceed to phase two and be ready," replied a voice in his ear that only he could hear.

A smile briefly crossed his face as he led the team deeper into the bowels of SI6.

Andrei looked at Sergei and said, "Good work."

"I told you I could intercept their calls, and my English is as good as a native of this Godforsaken land," Sergei replied proudly.

"I never doubted you. Now back to work," Andrei said, cutting him off.

They still had much to do.

CHAPTER TEN

A truck pulled up at the entrance to the underground facility that was the headquarters for SI6.

Out of the cabin jumped two men who walked around the rear of the huge container on the back of the vehicle.

The street was deserted, so parking was not a problem. The only witnesses to this event were the several cameras dotted about covering the entrance and delivering the visuals to the security desk inside.

The rear doors of the container were flung open, and men poured out in a flood of aggression. Each man was dressed in black combat fatigues and carried assault rifles.

The driver had walked up to the entrance and opened the door.

The guard was surprised by the intrusion. He'd watched the truck arrive and automatically sealed the door, but with no effect; something was jamming the electronic locks.

The driver took out a silenced Sig pistol and shot the guard as he was reaching for his weapon. The bullet fragmented his skull and painted the wall behind with his blood.

No alarm was sounded as the assault team poured through the now clear entrance. It had taken less than thirteen seconds from the arrival of the truck to them gaining access.

SI6 had been breached.

———

Jack asked, "Sir, just a question, but who authorized the access of the new security? Don't either you or Tony have to authorize any new details like that?"

Bainbridge looked at Tony, then at Jack, his eyes wide with understanding.

Before he could say anything, an alarm rang throughout the entire facility.

Jack had his Walther out the second he heard the alarm, his worst fears realized.

"We've been breached," Tony said as the shock passed through the room like a tidal wave.

John and Tony both had their pistols drawn and were ready, looking at the exits.

Jack said, "We need to get you to a secure location, sir."

"This is supposed to be a secure location, Jack," Bainbridge spat back.

"You can stand here all day and bollock me for fucking up and die when whoever has breached this place reaches us, or you can shut the hell up and let me do my job, sir," Jack snapped back, unfazed by his superior's anger.

Bainbridge nodded his head, his eyes still flaring with

anger but tempered by common sense. He knew Jack was right, and they had to work together to get out of this.

"Sir, head for the emergency exits," Jack instructed. To Tony, he said, "You stay with him, sir, we'll ensure you have a clear path."

"Commander, you're with me," Jack said, turning to John.

"What're you going to do, Jack?" Tony asked before moving off.

"Like I said, my job," he replied, then with a wave to John, he moved off towards the interior of the base.

The strike team moved through the upper levels of the base shooting anything that moved as they went. Anyone who stood in their way was cut down mercilessly.

Within a short few minutes, they had gained control of the top three levels of the base. Anyone who wasn't shot and killed was forced to retreat down to the lower levels.

The leader motioned for two of them to remain behind to cover their exit as they proceeded on to the basement levels where their target was.

Bainbridge and Tony were heading along a corridor when they saw a group of nine figures heading their way.

"General Bainbridge, we're here to escort you to a safe location," Inspector Smith said.

Tony immediately put himself in front of his boss to act as a shield should the worst happen.

"And you are?" Bainbridge asked over Tony's broad shoulder.

Viktor introduced himself as the leader of the Protection Command team.

Tony had his pistol up and aimed at Viktor's face as soon as he finished his introduction.

"Back off. We're going nowhere with you," Tony commanded.

The team fanned out, filling the corridor, and Viktor asked, "Where are you going to go? Have you enough bullets to kill all of us?" all pretense dropped, for he knew their cover had been blown. It was nothing they hadn't planned for though.

Tony gauged the eyes of the man in front of him; steely determination filled them along with a confidence that was slightly unnerving.

Movement at the extreme edge of his peripheral made him move his aim slightly, which was all Viktor needed.

Tony's arm was thrust up as his hands were gripped. The gun went off, the sound amplified in the confines of the corridor.

Suddenly the Inspector and another were on him. The leader of the team held his hands, thrusting them up and away from any targets as another grappled with him. Another of the team joined in, and he was struggling to fend them off.

He saw Bainbridge being held with a gun to his head and he froze.

"I'm glad you finally see the sense of it," Viktor said as he tore the pistol from Tony's grip.

Tony's face darkened with anger, at himself mostly, for walking into the trap. Obviously, the team had split up and one of them had hidden in an office and waited for them to pass to be confronted by the bulk of the team. As soon as their attention was focused on the bulk of the team, the lone man came up from behind and grabbed Bainbridge.

"If you harm him..." Tony left the rest of his threat unsaid.

"You are in no position to make threats, Colonel, and besides, the General is more valuable to us alive and unharmed," Viktor told him with a sneer of contempt. "If I were you, I'd ensure I was useful too, then I just might keep you alive a bit longer," he added.

"What do you intend on doing?" Bainbridge asked, his voice strained as he had a gun pressed against his temple.

"You'll find out soon enough, don't worry," Viktor teased. "Now move, we are going to the escape tunnel," he added.

Tony gave Bainbridge a pointed look. The escape tunnel was a closely guarded secret about the headquarters. However, seeing as how they had gained access to the base so easily, and that they seemed to know their way around it so well, it shouldn't really surprise them that they knew this fact too.

The man holding Bainbridge pushed him forward, toward Tony.

"Walk or die," Viktor told Tony.

"Retreat is the better part of valour, Tony," Bainbridge said, stopping his Chief of Staff from trying something they all knew had no chance of success.

"Just cut the quotes and move," Viktor said, which ended all further comment.

They all moved towards the escape tunnel.

CHAPTER ELEVEN

Viktor and the team reached the lowest level in the base and were faced with a wall that had a door imbedded deeply into it. At the side of the huge door was a panel; it was a palm reader.

"You know what to do. Don't make me chop off your hand," Viktor said coldly.

Bainbridge placed his right hand on the reader panel, and a blue strip of light traveled from the bottom to the top of the panel. There was an audible click, and the door slowly swung open.

Viktor said, "Target acquired, pull back to the evac location."

Tony followed Bainbridge through the door into the escape tunnel. The moment the door was opened, the light in the tunnel came on, illuminating the area. Shadows danced across the floor as they walked through the steeply inclined tunnel to the exterior of the base.

Jack stopped at the door to the level where reports had located the intruders.

Holding his Walther in both hands, he prepared to burst through onto that level.

John was facing him on the opposite side of the door, waiting for the signal. Jack was the lead man in this op, and he was conscious of the importance of the chain of command.

"On three," Jack said.

John nodded assent.

Jack counted down on his fingers.

When he reached three, he opened the door and moved through, scanning the opening with his gun. John followed the move copying the action.

The staircase was clear.

Jack led the way up to the door at the top.

Following the same procedure, they burst through the door onto the next level.

They were faced with a guard who spun and aimed his pistol at them both.

"Stand down," Jack ordered.

The guard lowered his weapon when he recognized that the two newcomers were not the threat.

"What's the situation here?" Jack asked as he looked around the corridor. There were two bodies lying on the floor and three more lying against the walls holding wounds and being tended to by other personnel.

"The hostiles pulled back a few moments ago, sir. I have no idea why, we didn't have the firepower to stop them," the guard reported.

Jack guessed as much from what he could see, but he had no idea why. He touched his ear bug and asked, "Colonel, where are you?"

When there was no answer, he contacted Deakin.

"Deakin, I need a location fix on Tony and the General asap," he said, emphasizing the urgency.

Deakin's voice came through immediately. "I have them leaving the escape tunnel with that extra security unit the Protection Command sent," he said.

"Are they safe?" Jack asked, his voice rising slightly in concern.

"It looks like the Protection Command team are forcing them into a helicopter at gunpoint," Deakin said urgently.

"Fuck! The Hierarchy have them," Jack said.

Tony walked out into the clean, fresh air. He saw the chopper come in to land, the rotors whipping the air into a frenzy.

He kept close to Bainbridge, keeping an eye on the men and women around them. He watched their faces, all hard professionals devoted to the job.

The man he knew as Inspector Smith turned to the two of them and said, "Get aboard."

With all the guns trained on them, they really had no choice but to comply. Tony knew if he got on board the chopper though, he would die. It may not happen right away, but there was only one way either of them would come out of this situation, and that was dead.

Bainbridge's only chance was if Tony escaped and lead the rest of SI6 in finding where they were about to take Bainbridge—and bring him back.

The nine figures formed a cordon around the hatch in the chopper.

Tony saw Bainbridge look at him, and in his eyes, he saw that he'd come to the same conclusion.

He nodded his head almost imperceptibly.

"Where're you taking us?" Bainbridge asked the leader, giving Tony time and space to move slightly backward and closer to one of the team.

The leader said, "None of your concern, just get on board."

"Of course it's my concern, you moron. I'm involved, aren't I?" Bainbridge spat back, unafraid.

Tony saw all the attention flow to what was happening at the front between Bainbridge and the leader, and he prepared to make his move.

"Get on board yourself now, or you'll be carried on board, your choice," the leader ordered.

Tony watched as three of the men moved closer in preparation to force him on board

No one was watching him; this was his chance.

As one of the men moved closer to him on his left, his attention was on Bainbridge and their leader. Tony grabbed the man's gunhand with his right hand and then smashed the point of his elbow into his face.

He ripped the gun free and shot the man he'd just struck.

Suddenly everyone's attention moved to him.

He shot the figure closest to the first one to go down, then another on his right. He moved fast, firing as he did so, moving back towards the door.

Bainbridge was out of his reach, but he saw him move too. He saw him lunge at the figure closest to him and grab a gun. He saw as he wrestled the gun free and then shot the figure. The leader reacted by striking Bainbridge across the temple with his own gun.

Tony reached the door as he saw Bainbridge go down, stunned from the blow. As he fired two more shots before closing the door behind him, he was confident they would keep Bainbridge alive, for now at least.

He sealed the door behind him, then turned and made his way back down as fast as he could.

Whatever they wanted Bainbridge for, they needed him alive, for the time being at least. That gave them some time at least to mount a rescue operation.

The only flaw with that theory was that he had no idea where they were taking him.

CHAPTER TWELVE

Jack went straight back to the Situation Room, where Deakin had been monitoring events.

"Any news?" he asked.

Deakin looked up, his face white, and Jack could see by his jittery body language he was terrified.

"They bundled the General into a chopper and took off," Deakin informed him breathlessly.

"What about Tony?" John asked.

"I'm here," Tony said as he entered the room.

"What happened?" Jack asked as he took in the worried look on the Colonel's face.

"I managed to escape from them before they got away. They were trying to get us both into a chopper. I know they want the General alive for the time being at least, otherwise they wouldn't have gone to all this trouble to nab him," Tony explained, looking at the faces of those present.

"Well, this was a well-organized affair, to say the least," Deakin observed.

Jack turned to the smaller man to ask, "Have you got a trace on that chopper?"

"The chopper took off and headed out of view of the cameras," Deakin said.

"What about CCTV footage? London has more than any city, so you should be able to get something?" Tony said.

"They only cover the city, not the area above. We'd need radar from an airbase or the nearest airport," John explained.

"Right, good point. Get on to Fairfax Airfield and ask them to track that chopper. I want to know where it's going," Tony ordered.

"I'm on it," Deakin confirmed.

"What about those bastards who invaded the upper levels?" Tony asked.

"It seems they arrived in a truck which was parked outside the entrance. They overpowered the guards and then systematically worked their way through the upper levels killing anyone who got in their way. As soon as you, Colonel, and General Bainbridge were captured by the imitation team from Protection Command, a signal was sent to them, and they retreated back up to the entrance where they departed in the truck they arrived in," explained Deakin.

"What are your plans, sir?" Jack asked.

"It's obvious, isn't it? I'm going to get Bainbridge back," Tony replied.

Jack saw the torment on the Colonel's face. He knew he was hurting over the fact he had got away but the General was still being held captive. He could see in his eyes that Tony believed he'd betrayed his boss by leaving him behind. It was something he was clearly wrestling with, a matter of conscience, but in his heart, he knew he had done the only thing he could. By leaving him behind and escaping, he made it possible to continue the fight and marshal their forces in a rescue attempt.

Tony saw Jack looking at him closely and knew exactly what was going through his head. It was a weakness he didn't want them to see.

"I'll be in my office, let me know as soon as you have anything," he said as he turned and left the room.

Jack watched him leave, followed by the eyes of all those present.

"Well, that was a complete and utter cluster fuck," John said sourly.

Jack turned to look at the former SBS officer and agreed. "Let's make sure it doesn't happen again."

The chopper flew away from the scene and towards the outskirts of the city.

Bainbridge was slumped on the floor of the passenger section, surrounded by the remainder of the team that had captured him.

He was awake and had been since shortly after take-off, but he kept that fact hidden. The chopper was too noisy to overhear anything that was being said, but he figured if they thought he was still out cold, they would leave him alone.

Frantically he was thinking of ways to get word to SI6, who he knew would be looking for him. Nothing he came up with seemed practical though, and it was discarded as quickly as it came to him.

For the time being, all he could do was wait and see what happened.

Andrei walked away from the small man operating the computer.

"Sergei, good work. Keep a watch on their signals. I want to know what they're doing now and what they plan on doing next," he said with a satisfied smile firmly in place.

"Copy that, sir," the small hacker said, his voice a little shaky.

"Pretty soon, they'll have where the chopper landed. It won't do them any good though, because by the time they get there, my men will have moved off. Then the fun really begins," Andrei said, not caring if Sergei was listening or not. He was lost in the game now; the game was everything, and it was one he was determined to win for the honor of his family.

―――

Jack and John were standing in the Situation Room, watching Deakin work his magic.

He was in contact with Fairfax Airfield, who were monitoring the flight of the chopper. Or so they all hoped.

"I've got some bad news and some more bad news," Deakin said as he spun around on his chair to face the room. He'd just ended his conversation with Fairfax, and it did not bode well from his expression.

"Just tell us," Jack said eagerly. He knew Deakin had a tendency to waffle on, and the fact Tony had left had not eased his nerves any.

"Okay, Fairfax picked up the chopper more or less as

soon as we got in touch. They know where they landed," the tech said.

"That's good news, surely?" John commented.

"You would think so, wouldn't you, but in fact…"

"Spit it out, Deakin, the short version, please," Jack interrupted.

"…they know where they landed, but it's in a remote location, and we'd never get there in time," Deakin said, nodding his head, trying to keep it concise.

"In time for what?" John asked.

"They landed on a private strip where they had a plane already waiting for them," Jack guessed.

"Exactly right, Captain Cross," Deakin confirmed with another nod of his head.

"So have they tracked the plane's trajectory?" Jack asked worriedly.

"They said it headed for the coast but then dropped off the scope. I'm afraid they lost them, sir," Deakin told him.

"Holy fuck!" Jack exclaimed angrily, turning away from them.

Turning back to Deakin, he asked, "Can you extrapolate a destination from the data Fairfax gave you?"

"I could try, but I'm not sure how accurate it would be."

"He's right, there's no guarantee they remained on a straight course after they dropped below radar. They could've changed course completely, and we'd be none the wiser," John said.

"Correct, but at least Jack's right, it's a place to start," Tony said from the doorway.

Jack saw him walk back into the room; his shoulders slumped in defeat and fatigue.

"I've just been organizing the clean-up," he told them.

"Seventeen wounded and five dead. It looks like Mike is going to have some company soon," he added.

"What about that truck that the strike team used, Deakin? Have you tracked that?" Tony asked.

Deakin's eyes went wide. "With all the chaos about them taking the General, sir, I never thought to check," he replied, his voice almost breaking.

"Get right on it then, Robert. If anyone can find them, you can," Tony said softly.

Turning to the other two men in the room, he said, "Jack, as soon as we have any idea where that plane was heading, I want you on its tail. Start off at the landing strip; you might learn something from there. John, I want you on the tail of that truck. I know we're short staffed, and I'm not asking you to tackle these missions solo, but as soon as you have something, call it in, and I'll organize some backup for you both. Are we clear?"

He received affirmatives from both men.

"Right, get to it then. Stay on your comms at all times," Tony said.

Jack remained where he stood, lost in thought.

"What is it, Jack?" Tony asked.

"Something that Deakin said just triggered something," he replied, looking up at him.

"What...triggered what?" Tony queried.

"Well, when he mentioned them taking the General, it got me thinking. All this was about getting him. The team from Protection Command arriving just after we got back from the scenes of the explosions, then that strike team attacking, it all ties in."

"I'm not sure I follow. Are you suggesting the explosions were set off so they could capture the General?"

"Think about it, it all makes sense. It's totally crazy, I admit, but it's the only thing that does make sense. They timed the three explosions to go off simultaneously so that us three would have to investigate, not one after the other but together. Why...because they know we're short-staffed. They know exactly how many people we have in the field from what happened in Scotland."

"So you're saying this was all The Hierarchy then?" Tony asked.

"Who else do we know who has the clout to pull something like this off? From what we've learned of them, which is very little, they're global and have been lurking behind the scenes for decades, maybe even longer than that. It stands to reason someone with that kind of longevity would have the collateral and resources to fund something like this."

"Okay, go on," Tony said.

"At the scenes of the blasts, they made sure we saw one of their crew, the red hoody. We gave chase and then bumped into someone who stuck us with something that implanted the tracker. That was so they could locate this headquarters."

"Why all three of us though?" John asked.

"Probably so they could keep track on all three of us later. They couldn't know we'd all three return together, so I suppose it was a case of hedging their bets."

"Makes sense, I suppose," John admitted.

"Once they knew where we were, they sent the team to pose as the Protection Command security detail, standard procedure when there's a security threat. Obviously, they were here to grab the General; the strike team was the diversion."

"Wait a minute, the General checked with Protection Command, they told him they send out teams as soon as a terrorist threat is announced," Tony said.

"Did he? I mean, was it actually Protection Command

he spoke to, or was the call hacked? If they went to all this trouble to plan all of this, don't you think they'd have thought of that? I bet they had someone intercept that call just to allay our fears so that the team could do their job without us guessing their real motive."

He watched the faces of those present as his words sank in.

"Tony, they've been one step ahead of us the whole time, don't you think we should at least try and get out in front?" he said finally.

"What you say makes sense, but how do we do that?"

"For a start, we somehow nullify these sub-dermal trackers they implanted in us. I, for one, will feel much safer knowing they don't know my every move."

"I can do that with an EMP. I won't need to surgically remove them then," Deakin said, jumping to his feet.

"Right, that's a start at least. What then?" Tony asked.

"Well, we do what you suggested, that seems the best way forward until we know their endgame. They took the General for a reason, and I've got a feeling they'll inform us all fairly soon as to what that reason is," Jack said.

"Okay," Tony agreed. "Let's do this," he said with a smile. For the first time since this had started, he felt they had a clear path forward. Only time would tell what lay ahead for them though.

CHAPTER THIRTEEN

Bainbridge sat in the comfortable seat on the Gulfstream G550 that had taken off with the remainder of the team involved in his capture.

He looked around the compartment where everyone was seated, studying all their faces. The fact that none of them were concerned about him seeing them told him two possible scenarios were in play here. Either they weren't bothered about keeping him alive, or he was to be handed off to someone else where there would be no chance of him divulging what he knew. Either possibility was not a pleasant thought.

He glanced out the window but couldn't tell where they were. They were skirting the sea and could be heading anywhere.

The man sitting opposite him was the leader. He'd been called Viktor by one of the others, but that was all he knew about any of them. One name, that's it. Not a lot to go on, that's for sure. This had to be a Hierarchy operation.

He had severely underestimated them. He had

believed that halting their mission in Scotland would've put a dent in their operations. He had been wrong.

Thinking their resources would've been stunted was another underestimation. Judging by what they had used to infiltrate SI6 Headquarters and the subsequent events that followed, it had been a huge operation.

If he got out of this, then a complete re-think would be called for on their intel about the Hierarchy.

"No point in asking where you're taking me, I suppose?" he enquired.

"None whatsoever," Viktor answered.

Jack arrived at the landing strip.

The chopper was sitting there, empty, as he'd expected.

There was a small red brick building with a tower sitting on top to handle all the air traffic. It was perched at the end of the single runway.

He couldn't imagine it was ever very busy. It looked rundown and almost derelict.

He didn't hold out much hope that he'd learn anything from here, but he approached the building anyway.

The paint on the wooden door was old and flaky, and it didn't take much to open it. Once inside, he soon found the stairs leading up to the tower.

At the top of the dark and dingy stairs, a door led to the control tower.

He drew his Walther and carefully opened the door.

As he'd witnessed from the ground, the room was in darkness. No lights were visible from anywhere, and the equipment was switched off. As he walked around the tower, it was obvious the place hadn't been used in ages.

Touching his earbud to activate it, he said, "I'm here at the landing strip. It's a dead end, I'm afraid. This place hasn't been used in ages. They must've just landed here and taken off in a plane, they left here for that express purpose. None of the equipment is working, so there's no way to track where they went."

"Check the chopper to see if they left anything that could give us any idea as to where they might have gone. In the meantime, I'll organize a full forensic team to sweep the place," Tony suggested.

"Copy that," Jack replied and turned to leave the tower.

Something alerted him to the possibility he might not be alone. A movement caught his peripheral vision down on the ground close by.

Most of the tower was made of glass, which afforded him a clear view of the surrounding area. It also allowed anyone below the same view of him, offering no protection whatsoever should those approaching below wish him harm.

He pressed himself against the only solid area in the entire tower, the door.

Hoping he was being paranoid, but knowing that recent events were evidence enough to warrant caution, he peered around the door to look at where he thought he saw movement.

There it was, he saw it clearly this time.

He counted three people moving towards the tower, each carrying weapons.

This had been a trap.

This was all part of the plan.

He was trapped.

CHAPTER FOURTEEN

Commander Dark saw the truck as he approached.

It had been abandoned in a warehouse district that had become derelict over the past few years as the industry had navigated away from the area.

He pulled up a few yards away from the larger vehicle and carefully got out. He had his Sig out as he walked towards the truck.

"I have eyes on the truck," he said.

"Proceed with caution Commander, no risks, is that clear?" replied the voice in his ear.

"Copy that, Colonel," he confirmed. "I'm about to approach so hang on."

He'd looked around the area as he got out of the car. So far, it looked deserted, but he knew that could change in an instant.

Holding his Sig out in front, he slowly walked across the space separating the two vehicles.

The cab was the first place he wanted to check. If anyone was still in there, he needed to clear it first. The rear compartment would come later.

As he neared the front of the vehicle, he couldn't see anyone in the cab, but he knew they could be hiding below the dash.

He snatched the door to the driver's side open, keeping his Sig trained on the inside.

The interior of the cab was empty.

"Clear, the cab is clear," he said for the benefit of those listening in to his every move.

"Check the rear compartment," Tony advised.

"On it, moving around to the rear now," he said.

As he reached the rear, he noticed the doors were ajar.

A sound alerted him to the threat, but too late to react. Gunfire slammed into the doors of the trailer.

John dived for cover, rolling on the ground under the truck.

"Taking fire," he said, his voice straining over the sound of automatic gunfire. "It was a trap," he said as he looked in the direction the shots had come from.

Tony was striding around the Situation Room listening to the reports as they came in from Jack and then John.

There was no video feed for either of them. There was no available CCTV footage covering either area.

"Shit, they chose their sites well," he muttered to himself as he strode around the room agitatedly.

When the report came in from John, he was waiting anxiously, and then he heard the gunshots over the comms.

"What's going on, John?" he asked.

He'd heard him say he was taking fire and that it was a trap.

Then the line went dead.

He spun around away from the speakers in anger and frustration.

"Shit!" he exclaimed. He knew either John's comm had died, or he had.

Jack was glad there were no lights on in the tower. The last thing he wanted was to frame himself in the window against a brightly lit room.

He had one chance of getting out of this with his skin still attached.

He smashed one of the windows near the front of the tower next to the door. Thrusting his Walther through the opening, he fired a couple of shots to discourage those outside from coming up straight away.

Then he ran across the tower to the opposite side, where he'd spotted a fire escape.

As carefully as he could, he opened the door and sprinted down the stairs.

Once he hit the floor, he pressed his body against the wall.

The three figures returned fire at the tower window where he had been several seconds before.

His ruse had worked.

They had no idea where he was.

He peered around the wall and saw the muzzle flashes of the three shooters. They were behind the vehicle they had arrived in, a large SUV.

Taking quick aim, he fired at the nearest shooter.

A satisfied scream of pain told him his aim had been true.

One down, but now they were alerted to his position.

Gunshots chipped away at the red brick wall he was hiding behind.

He guessed one of the remaining two was holding him down while the other tried a flanking maneuver.

He turned to face where the new threat would come from and waited.

The gunfire ceased for a second while the shooter changed clips.

He moved around the wall and saw the shooter with a new clip ready to slam into the butt of his pistol.

Their eyes met.

Jack fired, his three shells slamming into the torso of the shooter knocking him off his feet.

He knew he had a few seconds before the last shooter was in a position to fire.

Jack ran across to the SUV and got behind the far side.

Just as he got there, bullets slammed into the vehicle, forcing his head down behind it.

A quick check of his clip told him he had one round left in the breach. He changed clips quickly, inserting the new one. Now he had nine rounds with which to deal with the last shooter.

This one would be more difficult though. He was ready for him, so no surprises. It made the odds more even but nonetheless dangerous.

A fast salvo of bullets struck the SUV, forcing Jack behind it once more.

He looked over the top to see just where the shooter was standing, but he had retreated behind the wall once more.

Jack fired two shots at the wall and then waited.

The shooter appeared with his gun out, ready to fire.

By the time he realized what had happened, Jack had fired again.

Three bullets slammed into the shooter's chest in a mist of blood, sending him staggering back to land on the floor, dead.

It was over for now.

CHAPTER FIFTEEN

John returned fire from his low position under the truck near the rear wheels.

His shots hit nothing but the ground as he'd fired in haste without having time to aim.

He quickly scrambled backward, toward the front of the vehicle, hoping the shooters would remain at the rear of the truck, looking for a clear shot at him.

There were three of them; he saw their feet at the edge of the angle of his vision. They began to spread out, two of them moving to the side whilst the last remained at the rear.

If he didn't do something now, he would be trapped under there.

One of the shooters came around to his left side, positioning himself between him and his car. John quickly took aim and fired a rapid three-shot burst. The shells shattered the shooter's right ankle, dropping him to the ground in a scream of agony.

John ended the man's pain with a double tap, one to the chest, one to the top of his skull.

With his exit clear, he scrambled out from under the truck and sprinted towards the car.

Bullets whistled past his head as the shooter at the rear of the truck saw him escape and fired.

John skidded to a halt behind his car, then ducked down as more bullets struck his vehicle.

He caught his breath as he thought of what to do next.

"I've taken one of the shooters out," he said, relaying a sit-rep to Headquarters. When he received nothing back, he realized his ear bug had dislodged itself from his ear. It was still there, but a quick inspection of it showed it had been turned off. It must've happened when he dropped to the ground under the truck, he mused.

Replacing it and turning it back on, he said, "I'm under fire, three shooters down to two. It was a trap, they were waiting for me."

Not expecting anything in return from back at HQ, he looked for the remaining gunmen.

The situation had suddenly reversed. Now it was he who had the cover, and the two remaining gunmen only had the truck to hide behind.

John targeted the shooter at the rear of the truck. A two-shot burst propelled him back behind the large vehicle. When he appeared to return fire, John shot him with a three-shot burst that traveled from his arm across his chest, with the last shell bursting through his throat. He was sent spinning back behind the truck's container to land on the floor.

Bullets from his other side struck his car, making John duck back down as the remaining gunman joined the party.

Moving around to the front of his car, he kept low so the shooter didn't see him.

Peering over the bonnet of the car, he saw the gunman looking for him, keeping his gun trained on the last position he'd seen his target.

Coming up from behind the car, he fired twice at the gunman.

The surprise on his face was quickly replaced by fear and then pain as the two shells stripped the life from him. He fell to the ground to lie in his own blood, dead.

Looking around for further threats, John quickly assessed the situation as clear.

"It's done," he said. He took out his ear bug and realized it hadn't been switched off as he thought, it was damaged.

He took out his phone and called HQ.

"It was a trap, three shooters were waiting for me," he said, a little breathless from the adrenalin surge from the shooting.

"Are you okay?" Tony asked.

"I am now," he replied. "What're your orders?" he added as his breathing returned to normal.

"Return to base. We have to discuss what happened. I'll get Forensics over there to see what they can find," Tony told him.

"Copy that," John said.

"I can understand why Number One was so perturbed by this group's involvement," Andrei said as he put away his phone.

He'd just received word that the second team sent to kill one of the SI6's agents had been killed instead. Anger fared through him, but he was not surprised. This was only a test, after all, the first part of his plan to judge their worth in combat.

It seems they passed with honor.

"Okay, let's see how they fare on the next challenge," he muttered to himself.

He walked over to Sergei and said, "Right, tell them it's a 'go'."

CHAPTER SIXTEEN

"What the hell is going on here?" Tony asked as Jack walked into the Situation Room.

Commander Dark was already there, having arrived just moments before him.

"You got me, sir," Jack said. "None of this makes much sense to me."

"If they wanted to grab the General for ransom, why haven't they been in touch before now?" John asked.

"It may not be just for ransom. They may want to extract as much info from him as they can before selling him on," Jack suggested.

"You think this is an auction then?" Tony queried.

"Could be, but I don't get why leave the hit squads with the two vehicles unless it was to take out anyone who found them," John said.

"Anyone who found them? It was obvious we'd send someone out to each site; they left them where we'd find them anyway. This was definitely about getting revenge on us for Scotland," Jack said.

"If that's the case, then we can expect more of the same from them," Tony concluded.

Andrei stood in front of the camera, shrouded in shadow.

He signaled to Sergei to start the transmission.

"Sir, you'd better take a look at this," Deakin said as the monitors in front of the Situation Room came to life.

They all turned to look at the monitors in question.

A shrouded figure was standing there.

"What's this, Deakin?" Tony asked.

"Sir, I'm not sure. It's being transmitted on all our frequencies, blanketing them all," Deakin explained.

"I think we're about to find out," Jack said.

The figure began to speak. "I take it by now you're wondering what on earth is going on," he said, a Russian accent clearly audible. "You meddled in affairs that were beyond your understanding recently, and now it's time to face the consequences. If you haven't already realized, you have become targets for some friends of mine. As sure as a laser pointer highlighting a target, you have been painted, and just as surely, you will be hit. It's just a matter of time. Wherever you go, no matter what security precautions you take, it will not change the outcome. Your fate has been decided, and there is no escape. "

The screen went blank, and they all continued to watch, unable to tear their eyes away.

"What just happened?" John asked.

"We've just been put on notice," Jack said, turning away.

"So now we know," Tony agreed, "there's a hit out on all of us."

"Looks that way," Jack agreed.

"We can't allow this to stop us from finding the General though," Tony said, looking around the room.

"Why didn't they mention him? I mean, they went to a hell of a lot of trouble to nab him, so why not let us know what they intend on doing with him?" John asked, halting further conversation.

"If you ask me, it's so we have nothing to go on, and we have to focus on the fact we're in the crosshairs," Jack opined.

"Yeah, but why warn us? If they put a hit out on anyone wouldn't it be counter-productive to warn the target?" asked Tony.

That brought looks of concern from everyone in the room.

"It's all part of this sick game they're playing with us," Jack replied. "They want us wary, on the lookout for threats. That way, we'll be off our game and not looking for the General."

"You're right, Jack, very devious of them," Tony agreed.

"It's genius if you think about it. They wind us up with the threat, then throw assassins at us so that we're too busy to even think about anything else. Meanwhile, they're clear to do what the fuck they want with the boss," Jack said wide-eyed.

"You almost sound in awe of them," John observed.

"The thinking behind the plan, yes, slightly, I suppose, but the people who did this, not in the slightest. You have to respect them though. They're not the run-of-the-mill suicide bomber type of terrorist with an agenda; these are smart-thinking business people. They have a plan, and they'll stick to it. We just have to find out what that plan is so that we can disrupt it. That's the only way we'll get any headway in this. So far, we've been on the back foot playing defensive because they've been on the attack. They've disrupted our game by keeping us unbalanced. What we need to do is learn what they plan on doing with the General so we can disrupt their plan and we can then go on the attack, putting them on the back foot for a change," Jack explained.

"What now then? How do we learn what they plan for the boss?" John asked.

Jack turned to the smallest man in the room. "Robert, did you learn anything from that clip?"

"Well, they were clever, as we expected, re-routing the transmission through several servers around the world, and it was only a short clip so as not to give me enough time to work, but I did it. I got their IP address. I know where they transmitted from, but you're not going to like it," Deakin said, his smile of satisfaction rapidly fading when he saw their expressions.

"Where are they?" Tony asked.

Looking at the Colonel and with a shaky voice, Deakin told them.

CHAPTER SEVENTEEN

Andrei moved away from the camera, a huge grin of satisfaction across his face.

"That should give them something to think about," he said.

"What do you want of me now?" Sergei asked timidly.

"Get ready to move your equipment, the next phase starts in a few hours. I want everything set up and ready to go as soon as possible, and I need you on sight when that happens," Andrei ordered.

Sergei nodded and immediately began to strip down his equipment, ready for transport.

———

"They're where?" Tony asked, the words almost exploding from his mouth.

"Are you sure?" Jack asked.

"Are you disparaging my expertise?" Deakin snarled. Doubting his skill was the only thing guaranteed to get under his skin.

"Of course not, but we have to be sure," Jack said more softly this time, hoping not to antagonize the tech further.

"Well, in that case, I accept your apology. Yes, I'm sure I have my facts right. I traced the IP address to a computer; it wasn't easy. Whoever was behind this knew his stuff, he bounced the signal off a satellite and sent it around the world through several servers, but I got him. You can't escape from me once I get on your trail," Deakin was off on one of his soliloquies. Jack held up a hand, halting him and bringing him back on topic.

"Robert, short version, please," Tony said.

"Yes, sorry, I do get carried away, don't I?"

"Yes, you certainly do," Jack agreed calmly, hoping to get an answer soon.

"Well, they're here in a hotel in London," Deakin said. "The Burgess Grand, in fact, if you want, I can even give you the room number," the small tech added with a satisfied grin.

"It's a start," Tony said, adding, "Jack, I need you over there ASAP, find whoever's there and see if you can get where they took Bainbridge. Use whatever you need to get that information. Is that clear?"

Jack looked at the Chief of Staff and said, "Copy that."

He moved off, followed by Commander Dark. Within moments they were in a staff car driving towards the named hotel.

The short journey was completed in silence until they arrived.

"Okay, are you going to let me in on what's going on inside your head?" Dark asked as Jack pulled the car into the car park.

Jack looked at the Commander before speaking.

Composing himself, he said, "If this is the Hierarchy, then I owe them a debt that can only be paid in blood. One of their soldiers killed my wife and daughter right in front of me. He would've killed me, too, if I hadn't got the drop on him first. When we first learned of this group, we knew they were not your run-of-the-mill organization. We had suspicions they extended into lots of other stuff, but we never thought it would be this wide. This may be bigger than anything we, or any other service, has faced before."

"And you're thinking now you've bitten off more than you can chew?" asked Dark.

"There is that, but I have to pay them back for what they did."

"Jack, don't make this personal, or you'll lose sight of what's important, and what's more, you'll lose yourself in pursuit of the unattainable," Dark said.

"Unattainable how?" Jack asked.

"Well, let's say you get the man responsible for the death of your family, what's next? If this group is as big as you say, then who gave the order to kill them? If you get him, then there will be someone higher up the food chain, there's always someone higher up. What're you going to do, go after each one until you get them all?"

"If I have to."

"And what then?"

"I see what you're doing, and I get it, but what's the alternative? Just let it go?"

"I doubt that's possible, but what is possible and what's necessary is you have to move on. Use the grief to do your job, use it to keep sharp and focused, but you have to move on, or you'll end up in a downward spiral that there's no pulling out of."

Jack looked at him, eyes narrowing. He knew the

Commander was right in every way, he'd felt it himself, and it was something he would have to face at some point, but not today. Today he needed his anger. Finally, he said, "Let's do this," and got out of the car.

CHAPTER EIGHTEEN

The hotel lobby was wide and open, with a reception desk over to one side manned by two people, both young and attractive. It was tastefully decorated with wood paneling on the walls and thick carpeting. Comfortable armchairs were arranged around tables so that visitors had somewhere to sit and wait for transport to and from their destinations.

Sparing the receptionists a simple glance, they walked past them as if they belonged there so as not to raise any alarms.

Jack touched his earbud and said, "Okay, Deakin, we're here. Which room did you narrow it down to?"

"You want the third floor, room 316," Deakin replied.

Both of them walked through the lobby to the bank of elevators at the rear.

As one arrived, they entered, and Jack said, "Third floor, room three one six."

Dark pressed the button for the appropriate floor, and the doors closed.

The ride up was smooth and silent with no hint of

movement, and when the doors opened, it was with some surprise.

They exited the elevator into an empty corridor. Deducing where the room was, they moved in that direction.

At the front of the hotel, a large van pulled up, and a group of men disgorged out of the rear doors dressed in black combat uniforms, helmets on their heads, and holding assault rifles.

They stormed through the front doors and into the reception seconds after Jack and Commander Dark had entered the elevator.

One of them asked the two behind the desk, "Two men just came in here, which way did they go?"

Both receptionists were struck dumb by the sudden intrusion and were panicked into silence, simply shaking their heads.

The speaker indicated the elevators and the door alongside them that led to the stairwell.

Without another word, the group of five men burst through the door to the stairwell, rifles up at their shoulders, ready to fire.

"How do you plan on getting into the room?" Dark asked quietly as they approached.

Before Jack could reply, the door to the stairwell crashed open, and a group of armed men burst through, weapons up and ready to fire.

Bullets peppered the wall behind them, barely

missing the two agents who had been there moments before.

Jack grabbed Dark's arm and pulled him around a corner the second he saw the threat.

He had his Walther out and fired two rounds quickly around the corner after briefly glancing around it.

"What the fuck are SCO19 doing here firing at us?" Dark asked, dumbfounded. He was referring to the Metropolitan Police Armed Response unit, London's answer to SWAT.

"I have no idea, and we have no time to ask. We must get out of here and fast," Jack replied, his mind racing through the options. At the end of the corridor, there was an exit that led to a fire escape.

"This way," Jack said.

More bullets chipped away parts of the wall on the corner of the corridor, the sound of gunfire echoing in the confined space.

"Get the door open, I'll hold 'em off," Jack ordered. He pressed his back against the wall and, taking a deep breath, peered around the corner and fired off three rounds. The first hit the wall near one of the riot policemen's heads, sending a cloud of dust and shattered plaster into his mask. The second struck the man in his shoulder, sending him spinning into the next policeman. His third round caught another policeman in the faceplate of his helmet, shattering it and sending out a stream of blood and gore through the back.

Dark had the door pushed open, leading out onto a metal fire escape.

"Jack, come on," Dark shouted, "I'll cover you."

Jack turned and ran for the exit.

As he turned, his peripheral vision caught sight of a

small object that came tumbling toward the end of the corridor behind him. He knew instantly what it was.

"Grenade!" he shouted as he ran harder for the open door.

He saw the expression on the Commander's face as he ran towards him, eyes wide, mouth open, as he knew exactly what was coming.

Time seemed to slow as he ran, each step an eternity as he expected the world to erupt behind him ending it all.

He reached the exit and he slammed into the railing on the metal staircase. Dark closed the door behind him just as the grenade exploded.

Jack saw the door buckle in Dark's hands as he looked over his shoulder. The blast blew the door off the hinges flattening Dark against him with a bone-jarring impact that forced the air from his lungs.

Jack pushed Dark off him, and the door fell to the ground, tumbling over the railing.

Forcing air back into his lungs, Jack urged Dark down the fire escape.

Jack followed as the Commander rushed down the metal steps, desperately trying not to trip up. A glance up at the shattered door told him the police were still after them.

Why had the SCO19 been called in, and why were they after them? Two questions that burned in his brain. Answers to these questions would have to wait though, he brought up his Walther to fire.

He had three rounds left in his clip, so his next shots had to be accurate. If these were normal cops and they'd been tricked into thinking Jack and the Commander were terrorists, then he couldn't, in good conscience, kill any of them.

A face appeared in the doorway.

He fired one shot aiming at the doorway. The shell struck the doorframe sending out sparks as it ricocheted unpredictably.

The face disappeared inside once more, propelled by the fear of getting hit. It gave Jack the chance to continue down the ladder once more, but much faster this time.

As they were halfway down, bullets rained down on them, ricocheting off the metal stairs as it twisted and turned on its snakelike path to the ground, affording them a modicum of cover.

Jack hung tightly to the stairs until the blazing gunfire ceased. The moment it stopped, he leaned out and fired twice upwards, aiming for the shooter.

The Walther's slide locked open, empty.

The fuselage from above had stopped, either due to the shooter not wanting to get hit, or they were changing clips. Jack was not bothered about which it was, either way, it gave him time to continue to the ground.

He continued on his way and passed Dark, who had his Sig out covering him. As Jack made his way, he replaced the empty mag in his Walther with his spare, giving him another eight rounds of ammunition should he need it.

He heard Dark fire a three-round salvo just after he passed him. He got into position further down the fire escape and took aim. Dark followed suit and ran down past him.

They continued to the ground in this manner, covering for each other. Jack conserved his ammunition by only firing one or two rounds maximum. By the time he reached the ground, he still had three in his clip.

"Where to now?" Dark asked as he looked up to see if the police were following.

They were in an alley at the rear of the hotel. It ran across the back of the hotel and the other buildings in that block. A row of refuse bins were lined up against the wall at the back of them, which separated the hotel and the other buildings on this block with the buildings behind.

In his mind, Jack had the location of the car park where they had parked the car. He knew instinctively the fastest route to reach it.

"This way," he said, and set off running.

Bullets stitched a path behind them, closing in on their footsteps as they ran. Dirt spouts were thrown into the air at every bullet hit.

They reached the corner and turned towards the street.

Dark pulled up for a second, halting Jack with him. Jack took a deep breath, adrenalin still coursing through his bloodstream.

"What?" he asked, staring at the Commander.

"Would you send all your men up to the floor if you were in command of this op?" Dark asked, staring back into Jack's eyes. There was an intense quality to them, Dark noticed, he was exceptionally focused.

Jack glanced towards the street and then back at Dark. "I'd cover all the exits, including the fire escapes," he confirmed.

Touching his ear, Jack said, "We're taking fire here. SCO19 think we're the bad guys."

"We've been monitoring the event, Jack, and as far as we can tell, SCO19 have not been called out to your location. Whoever they are, they're not official," Tony replied through the comm channel.

Jack looked at Dark, "They're not SCO19, it's the Hierarchy," he said.

"How can you be so sure?"

"I'm not, but I'm certainly not sticking around to fucking find out," Jack argued. "Come on, let's make a break for the car park," he added, then sprinted towards the street.

CHAPTER NINETEEN

As they reached the street, gunfire behind them alerted them to the presence of the black-clad TAC team. They had reached the ground and were determined to stop them.

Jack whirled around and fired his last three bullets at the first man he saw. Only one of them hit the target, but it did enough damage by hitting him in his torso and knocking him over into those behind.

"C'mon," Jack said as he dodged past the corner of the building dragging Dark with him.

The slide on his Walther had locked open again; he was out of bullets and had no more spare clips with him.

"We have to get to the car. I have another mag in there," Jack urged.

Dark ran with him, glancing over his shoulder, ready to fire back if he saw the shooters getting nearer.

The entrance to the car park was at the side of the hotel and led to the underground parking area. They sprinted down the ramp to the floor where their car was parked.

Dark stopped Jack suddenly.

Bullets struck the wall close by, sending chips of concrete out in clouds of dust with every hit.

Jack went into a tuck and roll, ending up crouched at the side of a car.

"Shit!" he swore. "I need to get to the car for my mag," he told Dark as he came up alongside him.

"Get ready then," Dark told him. He winked his eye, then came up holding his Sig in a two-handed grip, resting his arms on the top of the car, and fired at the shooter. A quick two-round burst made the shooter duck behind cover, giving Jack time to sprint for his car.

He quickly got the door open and climbed inside. He had the glove box open in a flash as he reached for his spare mags. He rammed one in the butt of the Walther and the slide clicked back into place, ready to fire. He jacked the slide to inject a round into the breach and was good to go.

Outside the car, Dark was holding his own, keeping the attacker at bay. He'd continued firing at the shooter in short two-round bursts conserving his ammunition. As Jack exited the car, he saw Dark fire his last two shots. The slide on the Sig locked open, and Jack looked at where the shooter was. As the shooting had stopped, the attacker came from behind a concrete pillar to fire. Jack saw the move and shot him, his two rounds slamming into the top of the man's chest, sending him spinning to the ground.

"Get in the car," Jack ordered.

Before Dark could move, shots came from another quarter; ricochets bounced off the top of the car. Dark was near sending up sparks.

He dipped back down behind the car for cover.

Jack saw where the second shooter was and fired in

that direction. Both bullets buried themselves in the concrete pillar, showering dust and pumice on the floor in front.

"Move, now!" Jack shouted to Dark.

The Commander vaulted over the top of the car and landed agilely in a sprint for Jack and the car. As Dark reached Jack, more bullets struck their car; Jack fired back, silencing the shooter briefly.

Dark ducked into the passenger seat of the car, and Jack got in the driver's side. As Jack got the car running, Dark ejected the empty clip from his Sig and inserted a fresh one.

He drove the car towards the exit ramp swerving around corners with a satisfying screech of tires. Bullets peppered the back window, shattering it, and the two of them had to duck to prevent getting shot.

"Shit!" exclaimed Dark as he was thrown around by Jack's defensive driving tactics.

He struggled with the seatbelt as the speed and sudden maneuvers tightened the belt in its reels.

In a screech of tires, they were at the exit to the car park, the opening looming before them like the maw of some great ravenous beast.

Alongside the exit was the entrance ramp and it was filled by the black van that had pulled up outside the hotel.

As Jack drove their car up the exit ramp, a side door in the black van opened, and two black-clad men started firing Heckler Koch MP5s at them.

The steel-jacketed shells thumped into the side of the vehicle as it came alongside the van.

It was a service staff car, so it was bullet proofed. Although the bullets slammed into the side panels with a shuddering effect, none got through. It didn't stop them from flinching as the body of the car shuddered from the multiple hits though, a natural reaction.

Jack powered the car through the gate and out onto the road. Behind them, they saw the van do a handbrake turn as soon as it reached the end of the 'in' ramp and come after them up the exit ramp.

"They're not giving up," Dark said as he saw the van exit the hotel car park and turn after them down the road. He was twisting around in his seat to get a better view when bullets struck the rear of the car.

"You don't say," Jack said, glancing in his rear-view mirror. One of the gunmen was hanging out of the front passenger side window, firing an MP5 at them.

The effective range of the weapon was nearing its limit, so the bullets did little damage to the car.

"Robert, is there any way you can get these bastards off our tail? Innocent lives will be lost otherwise," Jack said through his comm link.

"We've alerted the real SCO19, but they won't get to you in time. Not now, you've moved away from the hotel," Deakin replied dourly.

"What about our own boys, surely we have a TAC team capable of handling this?" Jack asked as he drove the car through the traffic.

"All personnel are being tasked with securing the HQ. As you can imagine, after the attack, things are in disarray here," Deakin told him.

"Yes, yes, Robert, so you're saying we're on our own then," Jack said, shutting Deakin down from any further waffle.

"For the moment, I'm afraid so."

"Great," Jack muttered to himself, then to Deakin, he said, "Keep tabs on us and let us know of any hold-ups that slow us down."

"Copy that," Deakin said, then he went quiet.

Jack glanced at Dark, who had been listening in on the conversation. His pinched expression told him he wasn't happy with the outcome.

"So we're on our own then," he said.

"Yep."

"How the fuck are we going to hold off a vanload of mercs wearing battle gear armed with automatic weapons with just two pistols?"

Jack looked at him as an idea came to him. He smiled and then said, "We're not."

"We're not? What's that supposed to mean? I hope you're not thinking of giving up, 'cause these bastards don't look like they're the type to take prisoners?" Dark argued.

"Hold on," Jack said as he spun the wheel whilst yanking on the handbrake. The car spun around and ended up across the road, effectively blocking it.

Dark looked out his window as the van screeched to a halt, tires burning rubber.

"Oh shit!" he exclaimed, and then their world went to hell.

CHAPTER TWENTY

The side doors slid open, and black-clad soldiers burst out, MP5s up and ready to fire.

They opened fire on the car the moment their feet touched the ground. Bullets hammered into the side of the vehicle, rocking it on its wheels. The tires burst as shells ripped apart the rubber, the windows starred as the shells struck the bulletproof glass, eventually getting through.

The shooters stood their ground near the van, pouring more and more bullets into the vehicle until the charging handles all locked open. Flipping out the empty clips, they all reached for new ones. Pulling back on the charging handles, they began firing once more.

———

Jack dove out of the car the moment he pulled it to a stop. He grabbed Dark's shirt and dragged him out behind him just as the mercs opened fire.

Quickly he told the startled Commander what his

plan was. Getting a nod of assent from his partner, he turned and set off in a crouch.

Jack went right, and Dark went left, both traveling around their car and across the street. They angled towards the cars parked along the curb lining the street.

All the attention of the shooters was on their target, so they were completely oblivious to what was really happening.

Jack reached a spot parallel to the shooters on his side of the street. They were facing the car he and Dark had left behind.

He watched as they reloaded their MP5s then he made his move.

Two gunmen were standing on either side of the van in a staggered formation, side by side, with one slightly behind the other.

He moved forward, Walther extended, and fired. He fired at the shooter in the rear, his first bullet smacked into the side of his head, spraying blood over the side of the van. Before the man hit the ground, he was on the second shooter, who was just realizing what was happening.

Jack blocked the MP5 from being brought around to fire at him with his right arm and then punched him in the face with his left.

Staggered, the shooter's legs wobbled, and Jack shot him point blank in the chest while he ripped something from the shooter's belt with his free hand.

As the shooter fell back, Jack pulled the pin on the grenade he'd liberated from him and tossed it into the van.

———

Dark came from behind the row of parked cars opposite Jack and fired at the shooters.

His Sig bucked in his hands as the 9mm shells flew from the muzzle. His first three shots hit the first shooter, catapulting him against the side of the van.

The second shooter turned to face the new threat and was shot in the torso with three more 9mm shells before he could bring his MP5 around to fire.

Knowing what Jack had intended, he turned back to the curb and ran as fast as he could for cover.

Jack quickly turned and ran for the side of the street, away from the van. He threw himself over the bonnet of a parked car by the curb, landing hard on his shoulder just as the grenade exploded.

The shockwave from the blast rocked the vehicle he was behind as the fireball tossed fiery debris over the area.

Chunks of the van struck the car he was crouched behind with his arms over his head. The blast tore the van apart and anyone standing anywhere near it. Fortunately, it was only the mercs who died, any bystanders ran for cover when the shooting started.

When he was sure the scene had died down, Jack peered over the top of the car at the remains of the van. Just a blazing shell remained, burning away.

Across the road, he spotted Dark doing the same as him and waved him over.

"We'd best get going before the police arrive. They'll ask questions I'm not sure I can answer," Jack said once Dark had reached him.

"How, you wrecked the van with that grenade as well as our car?" Dark replied, looking grimly at the wreckage.

"I suppose we'll just have to leg it 'til we can pick up another form of transport," Jack told him.

"Copy that," Dark agreed, and the two of them started walking away from the scene of devastation before the crowds began to accumulate once more.

CHAPTER TWENTY-ONE

Once they were clear of the blast zone, Jack called in to base to give them a sit-rep.

"We need a ride back to base, the hotel is a bust. We'll never be able to get back there now, not yet anyway," Jack said.

"Jack, are you and the Commander alright? No injuries?" Tony asked.

"We're fine, apart from a few bruises. Nothing that'll stop us from doing our jobs, if that's what you mean?" Jack snapped back. He was feeling angry and frustrated at the situation, and unfortunately, he took it out on the first person he came across.

"I'll let that go for now and put it down to the situation," Tony said, "My tolerance for insubordination is limited though, Jack, so take heed," he chided.

"Noted," agreed Jack. "Any word on the General?" he asked.

"Not yet, and it's worrying that they've not got in touch with either their demands or threats or anything really. They just warned us that we're now targets," Tony said, his voice fading.

"What's the matter, Tony?" Jack asked, sensing something.

"Nothing, we need to find that plane. I'll set Deakin to work on it right away, you and Commander Dark get back here pronto."

Jack looked at his companion and said, "This is a total waste of time; they're probably long gone now. We've been ordered back to base."

Dark nodded. He knew this was bothering Jack more than he would like to admit, and there was nothing he could say that would make it any easier for him. He had served with friends who had gone through similar losses, and he knew from that experience that it was just something the individual had to deal with on their own.

"What do you think Tony's next move is?" he asked.

"He's going to get Deakin onto tracking the plane and see where they took Bainbridge. If *he* can't do it, then no one can."

"Let's hope we have some good news when we get back then," Dark said.

Jack agreed, "We sure could use some," he said.

"Is there no way to trace the plane?" Tony asked Deakin.

"I've got searches running for the plane's registration, sir. When it shows up, we'll know."

Tony saw what he was doing on the screen and asked, "What's that you're working on?"

"I'm running facial recognition on the people who came through that hotel I traced the IP address to, it's revealed some interesting results," Deakin replied.

"Wait a minute, how did you get their security feed? It's a closed circuit. Am I going to want to know the answer?"

"You asked the question, so I'm presuming that would be a yes, but as I'm saying this, I realize it was a rhetorical question, so moving on quickly, I hacked their server, which is directly connected to their security feed," Deakin rambled eloquently.

Tony turned away from the man hunched over the keyboard as he looked to the heavens for guidance.

"Deakin, that would be a 'no' then to my question. You had better not leave any trace of your activity there, or else we'll both be in trouble."

He held a hand up to prevent Deakin from arguing as he turned to admonish the Colonel about his ability and said, "Now tell me what you found."

Turning back to his computer with a scowl, Deakin said, "Well, I scanned all the people arriving at the hotel within the hours prior to the attack on us. I thought they would have needed time to set up and organize this, so anyway, I checked all the faces of those arriving after loading the software program. I linked that to all our databases, and it came up with some remarkable results."

A list of faces lined up above the live security feed still being loaded onto the screen and Tony looked at them all.

"Holy fucking Christ!" he blurted out when he saw them.

"Exactly my point, sir. I take it you know some of them then?"

"That's the crew that pretended to be from the Protection Detail, and he is Andrei Petrov, older brother to Grigori Petrov, who Jack and Mike killed in Crete not too long ago. He was the first link to the Hierarchy we learned about. He's ex-Spetznaz, a truly dangerous type. This is all his doing; he must be with the Hierarchy too. The other guy is Sergei Ivanovich, he's a tech genius like you," he explained.

"I doubt he's like me," Deakin chided.

"No, you're right, Deakin. He's probably better," Tony elaborated.

Deakin turned around so fast he almost fell off his chair. "What!" he shouted, his fists balled at his thighs. Tony had never seen him angry before, but his comment had had the desired effect. He knew now Deakin would go to any length to prove him wrong. He would double his efforts to find the General, triple his efforts if that was what was needed, but he would get the job done just to prove his status as the best in the business.

Fuming, the small man stared at the tall Colonel.

"Yes, you have something to say?" Tony asked with a straight face.

Thinking better of what he was about to do, he sat back down at his station, "I'll trace the whereabouts of this Andrei Petrov and his lapdog Ivanovich."

CHAPTER TWENTY-TWO

Bainbridge felt the plane's attitude alter as it reduced altitude.

Viktor had already closed all the window shutters so he could not see where they were. He would just have to wait until they landed to find out.

He felt the wheels touch down and the engines go into reverse thrust, the force pushing him against the seatbelt.

The plane came to a full stop, and he heard the engines power down. He unfastened his seatbelt and got to his feet.

Viktor remained seated.

"Let's get this done, shall we?" Bainbridge said.

With a smile, Viktor casually got to his feet and said, "If you insist."

The door to the Gulfstream was opened, and Bainbridge walked towards it. The scene that greeted him was not a total surprise to him.

"We're back where we started," he muttered, trying to figure out what their plan was. It made sense, considering the length of time they had been in the air. He had tried to keep a check of their flight, and halfway through it, he had felt the plane's attitude alter as if making a turn, and he had been correct. They had turned around to land back at the landing strip they had vacated shortly before. There had been just enough time to give those following the assumption they were taking him overseas, so whilst they would be chasing their tails looking for a suitable landing site for the plane, they had circled around and landed here. Quite clever, he decided, for it would be the last place they would be expected to pick.

A car drove up to the plane and stopped. Bainbridge walked down the stairs onto the tarmac of the runway, followed by Viktor.

He looked all around but could see no sign of anything remotely familiar.

"Get in," Viktor commanded as he opened the rear door to the black car.

Bainbridge complied; he had no choice in the matter really. He either got in freely, or they carried him in unconscious. He chose the former so he could keep his wits about him, he would need to know everything he could later when he made his move.

He sat in the seat facing the front of the car with two men facing him. Both had the Slavic features of broad faces and hard eyes. One was large, broad, and muscular, whilst the other was smaller with a wiry frame and wore glasses. He took him to be the tech guy, whilst the other was either in charge or simply the muscle. If these were Russians, then the muscle was probably in charge. It was very much a trial-by-combat method of advancing through the ranks in that territory, so it was more than likely that he was now in the presence of whoever had been calling the shots.

"Welcome, General Bainbridge. I trust your journey was comfortable," the muscle said as the door was closed.

Before Bainbridge could reply, the muscle turned in his seat and tapped lightly on the dividing wall behind him, signaling the driver that they were ready, and the car moved off. "I'll take your phone, please. Can't have you using it before the allotted time," he added, holding out his hand.

"Are you really interested, or is this what stands for polite conversation in your country?" Bainbridge asked with a sneer as he passed him his mobile.

"Ah, my accent gave me away, never mind. You are correct. In fact, I have no interest in your well-being, your comfort, or your health in as much as it will all change very soon, and none of that will matter anyway," replied the muscle as he faced him again. There was no trace of emotion on his granite features, just a dull look in his eyes. He had the look of supreme confidence those who had complete control of their environment wore when they knew nothing would happen without their express knowledge or say so.

"You think this," Bainbridge said, waving a hand around the car indicating it and the man before him, "will intimidate me, will scare me? You think you will scare me. What you do to me will instill fear in me? Go ahead, try and see what happens," he added staring right into the eyes of the man before him.

Dead eyes stared right back.

"You think you cannot be made to feel fear," Andrei said, leaning forward; it was not a question but a statement.

"When you've had the best part of you ripped apart right in front of you, there's nothing more that can be taken from you. I know, I've had it done to me," Bainbridge said.

"I know. I was the one who gave the order," Andrei said, sitting back with a smug smile on his face.

Bainbridge's eyes went wide as the words sank in. He was in the company of the man who had ordered the death of him and his family so many years ago. Had it not been for the timely intervention of his then-friend and now Chief of Staff, Tony Armstrong, he would have died with them too.

All the horror and grief of that fateful day came flooding back like a tidal wave of sorrow. It washed over him, engulfed him, threatening to drown him as his emotions were left raw and exposed. Memories of that day he thought he'd locked away in an impregnable vault, somewhere in his mind, were allowed to play. The vault battered open by this revelation, the sights and sounds of his wife and daughter lying dead in the back of a car assaulted his mind.

He felt weak, his breath gone as his resolve flagged. His vision blurred suddenly, surprising him, until he realized tears were flowing down his cheeks, his spirit broken as the death of his family came back to haunt him anew.

"Look how easy that was. Just one simple sentence, and you broke," Andrei smirked.

Bainbridge stared at the man, saw the smirk, heard the taunt, and wanted to rip him apart with his bare hands. Only a supreme effort of self-control kept him in his seat.

This revelation brought a new dimension to the entire situation, one that was as interesting as it was horrific. The Hierarchy had been around for longer than he had thought, perhaps longer than anyone ever imagined.

The attack on him and his family on the eve of him being given command of SI6 had been designed to prevent the implementation of the new unit. If he had died on that night, it would have set back the inauguration of SI6 years, if not decades. The attack had not been on him and his family, just him alone. His family had been collateral damage, and the man seated facing him had given the order.

What did that mean about his present position?

It meant that whatever they had planned, they thought it was close to fruition. He would not let that happen, whatever it was. He would find a way to get word out to his people so they could take them down.

The chances of him getting out of this were slim, and with this new knowledge, he deduced to do whatever it took to solve the problem.

As bad as things seemed, as low as his odds of survival were, he would not give up. He would not give them the satisfaction of seeing him broken and defeated. He would fight to the very last second, his very last breath.

When he felt he was able to speak, he said, "Do your worst."

"Oh, don't worry, I intend to," Andrei said with a cold finality that chilled Bainbridge's blood further.

CHAPTER TWENTY-THREE

"Have you got anything for us?" Jack asked as he and Commander Dark walked into the Situation Room.

Tony was still pacing the length of the room as Deakin worked away at his computer.

"We traced who is behind this. It's Petrov, or rather, the brother of the Petrov you killed on Crete," Tony said without looking at the two of them. He just kept on pacing.

"You mean *I* traced who is behind this," Deakin muttered, his attention seemingly focused on the screen before him.

Jack looked at each of them in turn, then said, "Is he working with the Hierarchy, or is this simply a revenge thing?"

"We can't confirm either, we just know it's him," Tony answered, shooting a sharp glance Deakin's way.

"Okay, so what's our next move then?" Jack asked, choosing to ignore whatever was going on between Tony and Deakin.

"Sir, I think I may have something, again," Deakin said.

Tony turned sharply to stare at the tech wizard and stopped himself from saying what was on the tip of his tongue. Jack saw this and guessed the two of them had just had a spat. He knew Deakin was extremely proud of his abilities and could act like a petulant child at times when he thought he wasn't getting the recognition he deserved. This was clearly one of those occasions. He also knew they didn't have time for any of this, so he intervened.

"What have you got, Robert?" he asked, softening his voice.

"I've been looking into Petrov and his finances, dealings, and so forth, along with his contacts. Nothing, but then it occurred to me, during all this time, we never bothered to check the General's comm or phone," Deakin said carefully.

The truth of what Deakin had said struck everyone in the room the same way.

"Fuck!" Tony shouted, "We've been that busy with the attacks on us that it slipped our minds," he added.

"I did say they were clever," Jack stated. "They're master manipulators. They kept us off our game so we'd be running around chasing our tails instead of doing what we should."

"Do it now!" Tony ordered.

Deakin turned back to his console and said, "Already on it, sir."

―――

Andrei turned to the smaller man in the car and asked, "Are they all there?"

Sergei looked up from his laptop briefly and said, "Yes, they're all there now."

Looking back towards Bainbridge, the large man said, "Say goodbye to your precious SI6."

With a nod of his head to the small man, Andrei gave the signal.

Bainbridge watched all this with interest. He had no idea what was going on or who they were talking about until he instructed him to 'say goodbye'.

What did that mean, he wondered? Did they plan on killing him here and now? But if that was the case, then why this whole elaborate scheme of kidnapping him, putting him on a plane only to bring him back to London? What was the purpose of that? Why go to all that trouble if all they were going to do was kill him? No, there was something else going on. 'Say goodbye to your precious SI6,' he had said, which must mean they planned on destroying the organization. How would they even go about doing that? He had no idea, but he presumed they were about to tell him, or was that part of the torture too, him not knowing?

He watched raptly as the man called Sergei did something on his laptop. What could he possibly do that could destroy SI6 from here?

"It's done," Sergei said without a single trace of emotion.

"Some say the world will not end with a bang but with a whimper. In your case, your world just ended with a bang, a very large bang," Andrei said with a grin.

———

"Okay, then where is he?" Jack asked as he leaned forward to look at the screen.

"He's right here in London, he never left," Deakin said.

"I don't believe it," Tony exclaimed through clenched teeth.

"Look for yourself, Colonel," Deakin told him.

"I'm not disparaging your expertise, Deakin, I'm declaring my own failure at not following protocols," Tony replied as he turned away from them all, throwing his arms up in frustration.

"It's not your fault, Tony. They had us running after our own tails most of the time," Jack said.

Tony turned to say something just as the room collapsed towards them as a series of explosions ripped apart the Headquarters.

CHAPTER TWENTY-FOUR

"And there you have it," Andrei said.

Bainbridge saw the man looking at him, gauging his reaction with those cold eyes of his. He had no idea what he meant though.

"And that means what, exactly?" he said more calmly than he felt. He had a sinking feeling in the pit of his stomach, like his world was about to drop away from him. He suspected the next words he heard would be the trigger.

"When I sent the team to attack your headquarters, they were sent as a distraction," Andrei said calmly, as if he was talking to a small child who needed things to be explained fully and simply.

"Yes, they were sent to distract us from the other team sent to grab me and my Chief of Staff...go on," Bainbridge urged.

"Not just that though, they had another purpose."

"Which was?"

"While everyone thought they were sent to kill

everyone there, I bet no one thought to ask why they pulled out so quickly."

"My people would assume they were sent as a distraction while the other team grabbed me, and once I had been taken, they would pull back. Job done, obvious, really."

"And quite right too, but they had another purpose. When you assumed at first they had been sent to kill everyone, you would be right."

"I don't follow."

"As they made their way through your headquarters, they planted bombs in strategic locations, bombs that were linked wirelessly to your computer network. You see, Sergei here is an expert hacker, and since this all began, we've been monitoring everything that went on inside your headquarters through your computer network."

Bainbridge struggled to take in what he was being told. Their network had been hacked? As far as he was aware, that was virtually impossible, but he supposed if someone could build it, someone else could tear it apart.

"You look confused, let me explain. We just set off the bombs in your headquarters. Everyone in there is dead."

Jack woke up to total darkness.

At first, he thought he'd gone blind. He was confused and had no idea where he was. The last thing he remembered was looking at the monitor screen before the room collapsed inwardly. He also remembered explosions.

Was he dead?

Was this what it felt like to be dead, he wondered, the absence of everything, feeling, touch, hearing?

He had not wanted to go out like that, but seeing as how he had, where was his family? Shouldn't they be here to greet him? He tried to look around to see if he could find them.

Then the pain returned, and he knew he was still alive, and the grief returned.

He tried to move and felt something slide off of his back. Dirt and rubble slid from him, allowing him some semblance of sight.

The room was in darkness, made worse by the dust that hung in the air like a cloud.

He struggled to free himself, feeling every muscle ache as he moved.

"Is anyone hurt, sound off?" he said, his voice coming out more like a growl as he forced the words through his dust-coated throat.

Slowly he began to see signs of life around the room.

Tony emerged like some monolith from beneath a pile of rubble, shaking dust and dirt loose from his massive shoulders. Commander Dark was next, followed by the smaller Deakin, who was groaning.

"We need to find out the extent of the damage and find a way out. Look for survivors as you go through," Jack said, taking control.

He went over to Deakin, who was struggling more than the rest, and helped him to his feet. He dusted him off and supported him. Through the haze, he could tell by the wide stare in his eyes he was terrified.

This was not what he had signed on for is what he would say, and he would be right. He was not a soldier like the others in the room, so he felt it his duty to protect not only himself but also others like him, the ancillary staff who, without their tireless efforts, this organization would not, could not function.

"Okay, Robert, take it easy. We'll get you out of this soon enough, but we have to find the others and make sure they're okay," he said.

"I'm okay," Deakin admitted bravely.

Jack saw Tony reach the door and force it open. All the lights were out in the corridor beyond due to an electrical failure probably brought on by the explosions.

"Commander, you're with me. We need to find a way out before this whole place comes down on us," Tony said.

"Copy that," Dark replied and fought his way through the rubble and mess to where the Colonel was standing, holding the door open.

Jack followed suit, helping Deakin by supporting him under one arm. He seemed to have turned an ankle, so walking was difficult. If the only injury the four of them had was a sprained ankle, they had got off lightly, he mused as he reached the door.

He propped Deakin against the wall for support and looked down the corridor. It appeared that the walls had remained upright, but ceilings had collapsed close to the blast site.

Taking out his phone to see if there was a signal, he said to Tony, "They'll send help, right?"

"Protocol dictates that in the situation of an emergency, the appropriate services will automatically be diverted to the location. In this case, we should have Paramedics and the Fire Service knocking on our door shortly," replied the Colonel.

"Right, we need to find out if there's anyone injured or dead," Jack said.

For the next few hours, until the Fire Service arrived

to dig them out of the remains of SI6, they hunted through the remains and rubble, finding as many survivors as they could. When they were freed, the tally was up by twenty-three to twenty-eight dead and many more wounded or injured.

As they moved out from the remains of the headquarters into the fresh air, Jack breathed in the still night air. The sun had gone down, and London was lit up like a Christmas tree on Christmas morning. He felt none of the joy that particular holiday brought though, because he was consumed by anger.

Twice now, they had attacked the headquarters, and both times, they had succeeded.

This had to stop.

CHAPTER TWENTY-FIVE

Bainbridge looked around his new surroundings with interest.

The car journey had been cut short when the large Russian received a phone call that seemed to make him sit up and take notice.

He had only heard one side of the conversation, but from what he learned and from what Andrei said after, their plan had altered.

The two attacks on SI6 HQ had been quite visible, especially the bombing, and the public were now aware of something terrible going on in their backyard, or so it seemed.

They had driven him to a rundown, seedy hotel. He had no idea where it was as the windows had been blacked out in the car, and they had placed a sack over his head to prevent him from seeing or being seen on the short walk over to the building.

He sat down in the only semi-comfortable chair in the room and crossed his legs, trying to appear as calm as he could.

"So what now?" he asked.

Andrei looked at him, his brows pinched as he thought about how much to tell him. After a short pause, he nodded, coming to a decision, he said, "It seems that your operatives are more resilient than I gave them credit for, and so I have called off the auction. I am now going with plan 'B'. This is a plan I have wanted to follow since being given this contract. I, like you and many others in our profession, must answer to our masters. After some persuasion, it has been decided that this is our new direction."

"Whatever you said must have been convincing, from what I gather of your masters, they don't like to be tricked," he replied, turning his head away in derision. He was pleased at the news of his men's survival, but he must not allow it to show. It was a tactic that Andrei saw through.

"Is it wise to try and anger me, to ruffle my feathers, as you put it?" he said, staring down at him.

"Are you actually asking my opinion, or was that hypothetical?" Bainbridge answered.

"For the moment, your co-operation is required, and it is only because of that you are still breathing. When it becomes no longer a necessity for your continued existence, then I can assure you I will put an end to it." Andrei stared into Bainbridge's eyes as he delivered his statement, and then, when he was sure the full impact of those words had been digested, he turned and left the room.

———

Jack, Tony, Commander Dark, and Deakin had remained at the headquarters, helping where they could and supervising the evacuation of the injured.

"What now?" Dark asked when they watched the last of the ambulances leave. The Forensic teams were already working on the blast areas looking for evidence as to what explosives were used and trying to find anything they could use to track and capture whoever was responsible.

Capture was the last thing on Jack's mind. He had another way of dealing with them, and it was definitely more 'Old Testament' than what had been suggested already.

"I suggest we all go home and try and get some rest. We can visit this again tomorrow when we are all fresh," Tony said.

"What about Mike? If we've all been targeted, then surely he will have been too," Jack said.

"It's all been arranged. While you and John were helping out down there," Tony said, indicating the underground HQ, "I called in a favor. He's being flown back to his old unit in Fort Bragg, where he'll be looked after in their hospital. It's probably the safest place for him to be right now," he finished.

Nodding his head in agreement, Jack asked, "When does he leave?"

"They said they'd send the ambulance around to transport him ASAP."

"Right, I'll make sure he gets to the airport okay, then I'll go get some shut-eye," Jack said and left the group.

There were plenty of vehicles parked nearby around the streets where the HQ was. He said to one of the Forensic team, "Throw me your keys, I need your car. Don't worry, I'll get it back for you as soon as I can."

"It's okay mate. I'll hitch a ride with one of the others," the tech replied as he tossed him a bunch of keys.

Jack caught it in mid-air and ran to the curb, pressing the button and looking for the tell-tale bleep of the alarm shutting off as the doors were unlocked.

Ten minutes later, he was pulling up at the hospital entrance. It was a Victorian town house with five floors and a large garage beneath.

Jack parked out front and ran inside, hoping he wasn't too late.

It was a private hospital run for the Security Services, specifically SI6. The reception was nondescript to keep with the illusion of it being a normal house. Further inside though, was a completely different story. It was a state-of-the-art facility with the best modern medicine could provide.

Jack ran through, signaling to the person sitting there that he was going to see Mike. As he opened the door, he saw his friend being wheeled out of his room on a gurney by two orderlies flanked by two men who were clearly guards.

The instant the door opened, they both turned to face him, guns drawn.

Jack held up both hands and said, "Take it easy, fellas. I'm just here to see my mate."

Mike raised his head to look at who his guards were aiming at and said, "It's okay guys, he's one of us, a good guy," then said, "Jack, buddy, you come to see me off?"

"You didn't think I'd let you get off without a goodbye now, did you?" Jack shot back.

"Can you believe it, they're sending me back to Fort Bragg, boy, the guys will sure give me some shit over this," Mike said, smiling painfully.

"Take it easy, Mike. You'll be back before you know it. In the meantime, I'll come with you to the airport just to make sure you don't get lost."

"I'm sorry, sir, but you can't travel in the ambulance with us. Our job is to protect Mister Flynn here, and there's only room in the vehicle for us. I'm sure you understand," one of the guards informed him.

"It's okay, I'll follow on behind. I have a car," Jack replied.

He nodded to his friend, and they continued on down the corridor towards the rear exit, where their ambulance was waiting along with the armed escort. Jack watched them leave before turning to return to his car. A feeling of dread fell over him as he felt something bad was about to happen, but he had no clue as to what, just that blood would be spilled.

CHAPTER TWENTY-SIX

"Sergei, send the transmission," Andrei said to the small tech wizard.

He had returned to the room where Bainbridge was sitting and had been joined by the smaller Russian. He had watched as he had set up his laptop and connected to the Internet.

Sergei glanced up and smiled, then set about doing something on his laptop that Bainbridge could not see.

He saw the smug little bastard glance up at him, and his blood boiled.

"What are you doing now?" he asked.

"Signing the death warrant on all your operatives," Andrei said with a cold finality that chilled him even more.

"Colonel, I'm picking up something being transmitted over the Internet," Deakin said.

He and Tony had reported back to a section of the

headquarters so far untouched by the explosions. Deakin had set up his computers and had started monitoring events once more. It was imperative they keep abreast of what was going on so they could inform their operatives. He rarely slept anyway, so he was glad to be able to get back to work. Tony hadn't wanted to stray far from HQ either, so he had gone to keep him company and see if there was anything he could learn that would aid their efforts.

"What is it?" he asked.

"It's them, sir. They're transmitting our location to every terrorist cell in our vicinity. Not just our location but photos of us, all of us, sir," Deakin said, his voice rising in fear.

"Shut them down," Tony ordered urgently.

"Working on it," Deakin said, his fingers working feverishly over the keyboard.

"Done," he said, flinging his hands up in triumph. "I terminated their signal, but I think some of it may have got through to a few."

Tony's face darkened, "How many?" he asked, afraid of what he was about to hear.

"Three, sir," Deakin said as he tapped in a few more keystrokes and then pointed at the screen.

"Those," he said, indicating the three hit men who the message had reached.

"Call Jack. Tell him he's about to have some company," Tony said.

Jack was following the ambulance in his borrowed car when his phone rang. He still had his ear bug in place, so he was able to answer hands-free.

"What's up, Robert?" he asked.

"Bad news, Jack, you're about to have some very serious trouble. Our details have been broadcast over the Internet, and a sanction has been put out on all of us. I managed to stop most of the transmission, but there are three hit-teams who got the word. One is heading your way. They're after you and Mike. Good luck, Jack," Deakin said quickly. He wanted to impart as much information to him as he could before events turned sour.

As Jack was listening, two motorbikes, each with a pillion rider on the back, came past his car at speed, cutting in front of him. They had placed themselves in between him and the ambulance, effectively cutting him off from it.

A third bike came past and slowed as it came alongside the ambulance. The pillion rider reached out and attached something small to the side of the vehicle, then it peeled off and accelerated in front of the ambulance.

"Holy shit!" Jack said, for he knew what was about to happen.

The limpet mine detonated, blowing a huge hole in the side of the ambulance. The force of the blast threw the vehicle sideways, tipping it over onto two wheels. The two wheels still in contact with the road continued to propel it along, but the center of gravity had now shifted, so it began to wobble before it finally tipped over.

Debris was scattered across the road from the crash, and several car alarms were set off by the shockwave from the blast that Jack knew would draw undue attention.

Jack threw his car into a sliding turn and finally managed to stop the vehicle across the road. His door was facing the ambulance and the two riders who had stopped as the ambulance tipped over. The riders were still in control of their bikes, keeping the engines revved and ready for a fast retreat, but the pillion riders looked at him.

He couldn't see their faces beneath the dark visors of their helmets, but he guessed they wore evil smiles.

Reaching behind them, the pillion riders brought out MP5s and aimed at Jack's car.

"Crap!" he shouted as he threw himself across the front interior of the car on his way to the other side. Just as he threw himself through the hastily opened door, he heard a barrage of bullets thunder into the side panels and door of the car as the shooters opened fire.

He had his Walther out as he got up off the floor and thudded into the front side of the vehicle. Aiming over the front end of the car, he fired a rapid double tap at the first pillion rider. The shells took him in the chest, knocking him back off the bike.

Jack turned his attention to the second pillion rider and fired once more. This time, the first shell struck him high on his chest, but the second smashed through the visor of his helmet before hitting him just above his nose. The twin impacts slammed him as they sent him flying off the back of the bike.

The bikes spun around, and the riders pulled out MP5s, too, and began firing.

Jack was forced to find shelter down behind the side of the car.

He could hear the shells pounding into the bodywork of the vehicle, and then the gunfire stopped.

It was what he had been waiting for; they were out of ammo.

He came up, targeted the first rider he saw, and fired twice. The rider threw up his hands as the shells struck him high on his chest, knocking him off the bike.

Jack turned his gun on the last rider and fired as he was ejecting the spent clip and was about to reload.

Jack's shot caught the rider in the arm, spinning him around off his bike.

"Fuck!" Jack snarled as he looked for his target again. The rider quickly got up, one arm hanging limply at his side and holding the MP5 out in his other. He pulled the trigger, and the gun went off, but the recoil forced the barrel up, sending the bullets high over Jack's head.

Jack's aim was better this time; his next shot struck center-mass, dropping the rider like a sack of shit.

He ejected the spent mag and replaced it with a fresh one, jacking the slide to inject a round. He was moving around the front of the battered car, heading for the back of the ambulance, keeping his gun trained on the bodies of the riders, when he heard the last bike come back. He was standing in the open with nowhere to go as the bike sped past the side of the overturned ambulance.

Reacting quickly, he threw himself to the side as the rider aimed the bike straight at him.

He landed hard on his shoulder as he rolled free coming up on his haunches. He still had his Walther and he quickly aimed and fired at the rider. His aim was to hit the rider controlling the bike, which would throw the bike off, and the pillion rider would be unbalanced, unable to hit anything with his gun.

The two shots caught the rider on the shoulder, sending him into a spin. The pillion was indeed unbalanced and tumbled off the bike, landing heavily and then rolling for a few yards.

Jack followed him with his gun, and as soon as he came to a stop, he was on target.

The pillion rider looked up at Jack, he had lost his MP5 during his tumble, and Jack could only wonder what was going through his mind as he watched Jack aim the Walther his way.

Any further thoughts were gone the second he pulled the trigger. The bullet hit him just below the collarbone, knocking him flat.

Jack quickly looked around for any further threats. When he was sure it was safe, he approached the overturned ambulance. He climbed into the back and saw the two guards lying where they fell. They had blood over them, injured by the blast. He checked their carotid arteries and was pleased to find a strong and steady pulse in them both. They were just knocked out cold.

Mike was on the gurney still, but it had tipped over in the crash.

"Mike, you okay, mate?" he shouted, and he was pleased when his friend replied, "Just about, buddy."

"Let's get you out of there and to the airport. Things have just taken a turn for the worse," Jack said as he righted the gurney and then set about untying the straps holding him in place.

"What've you got in mind?" Mike asked, his voice gravelly.

"We're taking one of those bikes. Do you think you can hold on the back?" Jack explained.

"I think we're about to find out," Mike said.

CHAPTER TWENTY-SEVEN

Commander Dark had left Headquarters behind on his way to his hotel. He had chosen one close to where he was going to work until he could find a more permanent place.

It had been a hell of a day, and if this was any indication of what life would be like working for SI6, then one thing was for sure, he would never get bored.

The hotel had a multi-story car park close by that visitors were given access to. He parked his car in the first available spot, not wanting to walk far, and headed for the hotel.

He was looking forward to a hot shower and a stiff drink before retiring for the night, but something was telling him that it was not going to happen. His sixth sense was sending waves of concern through him. He couldn't tell what was wrong, just that something didn't fit well with him.

Was it due to all the stress he'd been under since the attack and subsequent events, or was this something else? He was too tired to tell the two apart.

On his way over to the car park, he thought he caught a glimpse of a car tailing him. He changed his route and was rewarded with the suspect car continuing on its way. Of course, he could've handed him off to another car, but that would've meant there was more than one tailing him; a team that consisted of multiple vehicles, at least three different ones, and possibly a few bikes so the target doesn't suspect and never sees more than one vehicle.

As he left his car in the car park and walked the short distance to his hotel, everything seemed normal.

"Commander Dark, where are you now?" a voice said in his ear. He'd forgotten that he still wore his ear bug and was connected to HQ.

"Approaching my hotel, why?" he replied, suddenly going back on high alert.

"Three hit teams have been given our details and are coming for us. You have to watch your back, John. Get somewhere safe until back-up can be arranged," Tony said.

"When you say 'us', what exactly do you mean?" Dark asked as he quickened his pace towards the hotel.

"Our location and personnel files have been given out over the Internet. Jack, Mike, yourself, Robert, and I have all been targeted. We managed to prevent it getting any further, but not before three teams were alerted and took up the sanction," Tony explained.

"This Hierarchy sure aren't pulling any punches, are they?" Dark commented.

"If their intention is to keep us off balance, they've succeeded so far. We've not had time to re-group or even think of what to do next before they hit us with something new. We need to stop them before this gets out of hand," Tony said.

"Well, considering what they've done so far, I don't think I want to know what you call 'out of hand'," Dark quipped.

"Just get somewhere safe, John. I'll try and organize some backup," Tony said.

"Copy that. Keep me informed on who you send and when. We don't want them getting shot when they only want to help," Dark said.

He continued walking, watching the streets for any signs that he was being tailed. He was on high alert, all tiredness evaporated with the news from Tony. He was boosted by the confidence that carrying his Sig gave him. If they came for him, they would not take him without a fight.

Something out of the corner of his eye caught his attention.

A motorbike rushed past but seemed to slow as it passed him, and then it was gone.

A spotter, he thought.

He had to move fast and get to cover. They would be here soon, he knew.

Just as he quickened his pace, a black Transit van came hurtling down the street. A side panel door opened, and he saw a man kneeling in the space holding an MP5.

"Oh crap!" he said as his world turned to hell once more.

CHAPTER TWENTY-EIGHT

Jack steered the stolen bike through the streets, hoping the police didn't pick him up. He hoped they would be too busy investigating the crime scene he had just vacated to worry about chasing him.

Mike was holding on to him, leaning into his back to streamline their profile and help keep the bike upright.

He knew his friend was still weak from his recent operations and sustained injuries from the recent action in Scotland, which was all the more reason to get him to his plane and to safety.

He felt Mike turn his head away from his back. He knew instinctively what he'd seen.

Somehow they were on to them again.

It seemed whoever was after them had an endless supply of operatives to throw at them to ensure the job got done.

He swerved the bike around several cars on the road. Even at this late hour, the traffic was busy. Then again, it was London.

In the side mirrors, he saw two cars follow him

around the vehicles he'd just passed and knew it was them.

Putting his head down, he accelerated even faster, pushing the bike close to sixty miles per hour. In this traffic, on these streets, it was almost suicidal. It was something he had to do though, if he wanted to escape.

Bullets zinged off the surface of the road as they tried to intimidate him.

He zigzagged out of the path, causing the bike to wobble a little. He got it back under control and opened it up for even greater speed.

With Mike holding on in his weakened state and him concentrating on controlling the bike, there was nothing either of them could do to deter them from shooting at them. The only thing he could rely on was speed and the impressive maneuvering capabilities of the bike.

His destination was RAF Northolt, where military transport was waiting to take Mike to Fort Bragg. If he could just get close enough, the MPs would help out with their little problem.

Another barrage of bullets flew past the bike. A stray round snapped off the wing mirror near Jack's right hand. He jinked the handlebars to the left, startled by how close it had come, and almost lost control. The bike swerved across the road into the path of an oncoming taxi. Jack had to mount the curb on the opposite side of the road to evade being knocked off the bike by the onrushing vehicle.

Bystanders ran for cover as he rushed towards them. As bullets pinged off walls, Jack fleetingly saw people dash behind parked cars or rush into doorways cowering close to anything that would protect them from the hailstorm raining down on them.

Swerving back onto the road, narrowly missing another vehicle, Jack powered the bike up the road again.

The two cars chasing them increased their speed to keep up. Because of his diversion onto the curb, one of the cars was able to catch up. It came alongside them.

"Jack!" Mike warned.

"I know, I'm on it," Jack replied, shouting so he could be heard over the engine noise as he pushed it up, close to its limits.

Jack reached for his Walther, keeping it hidden from the car alongside. He made sure the road ahead was clear, then turned to look at the driver in the car to his left and fired. Three rounds hit the side window shattering the glass as they punched through to hit the driver in the head and neck.

The car suddenly lost control as the driver slumped over the wheel.

Jack returned his Walther to his holster and then opened up the throttle, powering forward.

The car behind swerved across the road, crashing into a parked car at the side. The following car, unable to avoid it, ran into the rear quarter, coming to a halt.

In his one remaining wing mirror, Jack saw the men get out of the cars and fire down the road at them. Jack kept his head down and pushed the throttle open even more. He knew he was probably out of range, but he was taking no chances on Mike getting hit behind him.

As he steered the bike around a corner, he knew they were clear. All they had to do now was make Northolt, and this part of the mission would be complete; Mike would be safe, and he could return to finish off the job.

CHAPTER TWENTY-NINE

Dark dived for cover behind the nearest parked car.

Bullets thudded into the vehicle as the MP5 unloaded its clip into it.

Dark had his Sig out and ready to fire, he just needed the opportunity.

The fuselage finished, out of ammo. Dark knew they would need a few seconds to reload. This was his chance.

He came up holding the Sig out in both hands. He quickly took aim and fired a three-round salvo.

Satisfaction bloomed in him as he saw the shooter knocked back into the van as his three rounds slammed into him.

Before anyone else could join the fray, Dark targeted the driver and fired two shots. He saw the bullets slam into the window forming starburst patterns as they passed through. He saw the driver slump forward as blood bloomed on the window from the hits.

Doors on the other side of the van were quickly opened, and men poured out, at least three more armed with MP5s.

Dark knew he was outgunned. He had to act fast if he wanted to survive the next few minutes.

The first man he saw, he fired at. Three rounds caught him high on the chest, knocking him flat. The other two scattered, each going in opposite directions, making it harder for Dark to fight.

He moved back down the road, angling to get around the front of the van. He knew if there was anyone still inside, they were probably unarmed, or they would've already joined the fight. That being said, the three that got out of the van were still too many to handle on his own. He would need a whole lot of luck to get out of this alive, or incompetency on their part.

The first gunman showed himself immediately, running around the van and straight onto the pavement. Dark saw him and fired two shots that dropped him like a stone.

One down, perhaps these weren't as good as he'd feared.

Bullets pinged off the concrete of the pavement as the other two gunmen opened fire.

Dark was crouched behind a parked car, so they had no line of sight on him and were firing blindly. The fear of seeing their comrade going down sent them into panic.

Dark worked his way to the front of the van, leaving the two gunmen looking for him from the rear of the vehicle.

Seeing his chance, he ran for the cover of the large vehicle. In the distance, he could hear sirens blaring as the police were on their way. He had to finish this first though, before they intervened and mistook him for one of the bad guys.

Keeping low, he worked his way up the side of the van, facing the road towards the back of the van. He peered around the edge to see the two gunmen looking down the pavement for him.

"Boo!" he said.

The two gunmen turned around, startled by his appearance. Their submachine guns were lowered, and by the shocked looks on their faces, he knew they would make a move against him.

He already had his Sig aimed at them.

"Don't do anything stupid, you two," he warned.

They went for it anyway.

Dark shot each of them as they tried to bring up the MP5s to fire; he had no choice.

"Fuck! Damn and blast!" he shouted as he saw them drop.

He covered the van and then checked inside to ensure no more threats were lurking inside. It was clear, as he'd suspected, he'd killed the driver earlier.

He touched his earbud to activate the comm. "Tony, scratch one hit-team. I'm returning to base, or what's left of it. This is far from over," he said.

CHAPTER THIRTY

Bainbridge sat seething as he contemplated what was going on out in the city.

There was nothing he could do at the moment to help or prevent things from escalating further, and it did not sit well with him.

Andrei was standing over by the window, staring out at the city below, his hands behind his back. A ringtone rang out over by the window. Bainbridge looked to where the sound originated from, for he recognized that certain tone.

Andrei looked down at his jacket pocket and reached a hand inside to withdraw the phone. He looked at the caller ID and then over at the man seated looking at him.

"I think you're going to want to take this call," he said, tossing Bainbridge the phone.

As he looked at the small screen, he understood. Now all the pieces seemed to fit.

Was this what the Hierarchy was after all along? Could it all be that simple? He would have to play along to find out.

He put the phone up to his ear and said, "Yes, Prime Minister, what can I do for you?"

Tony received the call from Dark and was relieved to some extent.

He looked at Deakin, who had been listening in. Jack had called in that Mike had been dropped off at RAF Northolt and he was returning to base also. The look of concern on his face was enough for Deakin to ask, "You don't think the third team will come here, do you, Colonel?"

"If I've learned anything in this life, Robert, it's not to take anything for granted," Tony replied.

"But we've got staff all over the place, paramedics, fire service, and extra security. How could they possibly get in here?" Deakin asked, a note of derision in his voice.

"You've been so busy on your computers, you probably didn't notice everyone left almost an hour ago. The site has been secured, so theoretically, no one should be able to get in here. I doubt a string of tape would prevent a determined assassin though. The security is non-existent, they've been called to all the other incidents around the city. Basically, we're on our own," Tony explained bluntly.

He saw the color drain from Deakin's face as he swallowed.

"Looks like my promising career in IT security might not be as long as I'd hoped," Deakin said bravely.

"You stay here, I'll secure the door so no one can get in, and you keep working. Find everything and anything that can help us. I'll go take a look around and make sure the area is secure."

He knew he had to do something; he couldn't just wait for them to come to them. Before Deakin could argue, he opened the door and looked outside. The corridor was clear, littered with debris from the explosions, but no one was around. He glanced back at Deakin and said, "Keep working, Robert, you're the only one who can find what we need. I'll be back shortly." Then he left, locking the door behind him.

He found his way to the Armoury, where stacks of weapons had been tipped over and were littering the floor. He chose a pistol he was familiar with, a Sig P226, and a magazine holding ten rounds of 9mm. He inserted it into the butt and jacked the slide. He found another spare, full magazine and put it in his pocket, placing the Sig in his belt at the small of his back, freeing up both hands.

He left the Armoury and headed back to where he'd left Deakin.

"I'm picking up something that might interest you, Colonel," the tech said as he walked through the door.

"I hope it's good news, we certainly could use some."

"I'll let you decide."

Tony walked over to where Deakin was working and stood at his shoulder, looking down at his monitor.

"What have you got?"

"I've been monitoring some signals and communications played out over the last few minutes, and it seems there's a call for a meeting of COBR over the recent attacks and gun battles throughout the streets."

"If that's true, then they'll want the General in attendance," Tony said. "Can you monitor his phone?"

"He still has it on him, and it's still active. I'm surprised they didn't throw it away the first chance they had. They must know we can track the GPS on it."

"Perhaps that's why they kept it on him. I doubt anyone as sophisticated as Petrov would overlook something as basic as allowing a phone to be kept. There has to be a reason why they allowed him to keep it, and perhaps it has something to do with COBR."

"You don't think they'd try to attack that, do you? They'd have to be insane to even think they could pull something like that off."

Tony nodded his head, "I agree, but from what we've seen so far, I wouldn't put anything past them. They are certainly determined and audacious enough to attempt anything."

"Attempt what?" a voice asked from the door.

Tony turned to see Jack standing there; he looked more tired than he'd ever seen, yet with a dark, fierce intensity to his eyes. He knew this man was bordering on his limit, and he dared not think of what he was capable of once he reached them or, perish the thought, went beyond.

"We're just discussing a development Deakin came up with," he said.

"You mean why did they allow Bainbridge to keep his mobile? I wondered about that too."

Jack walked slowly into the room.

"Has it made or received any calls in the last few minutes?" he asked.

Deakin looked at his screen once more, then input more commands, and another screen flashed up on the monitor.

"Yes, he just received one, and you're not going to believe who from," he said a little breathlessly.

"The Prime Minister?"

Deakin turned around, his eyes wide, "How did you know?"

"It's beginning to all make sense now," Jack started.

Tony picked up on what he was going to say.

"You're suggesting that all this was a ploy to maneuver us all into a position where this would happen?"

"What position, what ploy? What're you two talking about?" Deakin looked from one to the other as if watching a tennis match, his eyes wide with wonder.

Jack looked at the colonel, "Think about it, why else would they go to all that trouble to capture the General? Why keep his phone, and why else would they put out that sanction on all our heads?

"They clearly wanted revenge for our intervention in Scotland."

"But if they wanted revenge, did they have to make such a show of it? All this was the opening act where we are all unwitting players. Think about it, Tony. This Hierarchy claim to have lived in the shadows for who knows how long. Now all of a sudden, they are perpetrating acts of violence throughout the streets of London like some crazed jihadist. Does that sound to you like a group that lurks in the shadows?"

Deakin followed where this thread was going, "Are you saying this isn't the Hierarchy?"

"No, I'm saying they planned this as a distraction to keep us busy and to get the attention of a certain individual. That individual has just made the phone call they were waiting for. If they got rid of us in the meantime, it was a bonus."

Deakin said, "You're not suggesting they're going to attack COBR, surely?"

"Just the opposite, in fact. I think they'll maneuver the Prime Minister away to some isolated safe house where he'll be more vulnerable."

Tony turned to the seated man, "Robert, keep watching the General's phone. If they leave it on, I want to know where they're going."

Deakin returned his attention to his work, all his focus on what he was monitoring.

Tony looked at Jack, his eyes dark. "Do you really think they're going after the Prime Minister?"

"It all makes sense now: the attacks on us were nothing more than a diversion, a build-up to this one event. Isolate him, then kill him in a public way to throw the government into chaos and, with the same blow, destroy the credibility of all the Security Services. They would have to disband SI6 at the very least because it was Bainbridge who lured him into the target zone."

"Wow, this place is a mess," a voice said from the doorway.

They both turned to see Dark standing there.

"You know, anyone could just walk in here like I just did." He saw them glance across at each other.

"What did I miss?" he asked.

CHAPTER THIRTY-ONE

Bainbridge handed the phone back to the tall Russian. The entire time he had been talking with the Prime Minister, he had a gun aimed right at his face, ensuring he said the right thing at all times. It was a testament to his being able to handle pressure that he was able to pull this off without alerting the man on the other end to his predicament.

"Very good, General. I must say, you handled that with panache," Andrei congratulated as he took the phone. He put away his gun and pocketed the phone once more.

Looking at Sergei, he asked, "Was it intercepted?"

The other smiled and nodded his head.

"Good. Contact Viktor and tell him things are moving along nicely. Give him the location and tell him to be ready."

"Copy that," Sergei replied.

"You're mad, you know that, don't you? You can't seriously think you'll get away with this?" Bainbridge questioned.

"Get away with what, may I ask? You have no idea what my intentions are."

"Well, let me see, you intend on luring the British Prime Minister to his death at the secluded safe house we just arranged during that call, that much is a given. I don't have to be a genius to have worked that one out."

"Bravo, General. I'm so glad you were able to keep up."

"I try. What I don't understand though, is why. Why all this show if your intention was to kill the Prime Minister all along? Surely even a man of your limited intelligence could have come up with a better plan than this."

Sergei spun around from what he was doing to stare at the two of them. His eyes immediately went to Andrei, who he knew had a violent temper, and then to Bainbridge, who wore a slight smile.

"Again, you try to goad me into a show of anger, General. I'm disappointed, I thought better of you, but it does show me how desperate you are."

Sergei turned back to his monitors; the show he expected was not going to happen.

"And you have evaded my question once more," Bainbridge insisted.

"Well then, seeing as how you consider yourself so much more intelligent than I, I'm sure you will figure it out," Andrei said with a satisfied smile.

"Oh, I think I have," Bainbridge started. "It was a fellow countryman of yours, Lenin, who once said, 'the purpose of terrorism is to terrorize' that is what you're doing. You hope your attacks, which are merely a prelude to this attempt to kill the Prime Minister, will disrupt the normal daily lives of those people living in London. It will cause chaos and force the authorities to take drastic security measures to ensure something like this never happens again. You plan on killing the PM in a public display of force in a supposed safe location, further proving the security forces are not doing their jobs adequately, a shock tactic to ensure raised measures of security around the country. How am I doing so far?" he said with a smile as he watched the Russian's smirk slowly vanish.

The Russian turned away from him as he thrust his hands deep into his pants pockets so no one could see him clench them in anger.

"I presume, from your petulant air, that I got it right," Bainbridge goaded.

"You may have figured part of it out, but there is no way you could ever prevent it from happening," Andrei snapped back over his shoulder.

"You underestimate my men."

Andrei spun back around, eyes blazing in fury. "No, you overestimate them. Did they prevent my team from invading your headquarters? Did they prevent any of the attacks that set up this event? Did they even prevent my men from taking you right from under their very noses? The answer you're struggling to find, my dear friend, is 'no', they did not. They will not prevent the rest of my plan from being fulfilled either. You have played your part in this, and the only reason I'm keeping you alive, is for my pleasure, so I can gloat as I watch you when all this is done, knowing you could do nothing to stop us, but that could change. Sergei, if he opens his mouth again, shoot him," he said, then turned and left the room.

Bainbridge saw the smaller Russian look at him, a sneer stretching his thin lips as he took pleasure watching him being put down. Sergei returned his attention to his monitors once more, leaving Bainbridge to sit, wonder, and hope. He hoped his men were as good as he'd boasted and had also figured out what was to happen, or he could see this dastardly plot actually work.

"Is the trace still active on his phone?" Tony asked.

Deakin simply nodded as if the question was an insult to his ability.

"We know where they're going now, there can only be one place," Jack observed over Deakin's shoulder.

Tony looked at Jack, "Are you sure about this?"

Jack stood up straight and looked at him. "There's no other way."

Tony sighed, "Okay, let's do this."

CHAPTER THIRTY-TWO

Bainbridge looked out of the window as they drove up the winding, tree-lined driveway.

The house was situated on three acres of land, with a perimeter of trees that acted as a deterrent to any onlookers. Well-tended lawns spread out on either side of the looping drive as they approached the house. It was a three-story Victorian property previously owned by a member of the House of Lords who had ties to the intelligence community. Since his death, it had been used as a top-level safe house. It maintained a year-round staff of three maids, a butler, four kitchen staff, and four security personnel.

"I'm impressed," Andrei said with a smile as he looked through the front windscreen of their car.

Turning around to look at Bainbridge, he said, "Your decadent upper-class hierarchy is no different than our Oligarchs, I think?"

"Something we can agree upon, I suppose."

"Well, enjoy your time here, it could well be brief,"

Andrei said with a sneer as he turned to face the front once more.

The car pulled up in front of the huge house, and Andrei got out, indicating for Bainbridge to follow. Another vehicle pulled up behind them, a large SUV. Several large men got out and walked over to them.

"Viktor, glad you could make it," Andrei said to the man in front.

The doors opened, and the butler greeted them. "I wasn't aware anyone was due today, sir?"

"It's a special meeting with the Prime Minister, Watson. He'll be along shortly. These people are with me," Bainbridge told him.

"Just as soon as I follow protocol and verify their clearance, you'll be free to enter, sir," Watson said and made to return inside when a soft 'Pfhut!' was heard close by Bainbridge's ear. A mist of blood surrounded where the bullet hit the butler high on his chest, knocking him over into the huge double doors.

Bainbridge was about to say something when silenced weapon fire cut down the security guards who came to the butler's aid.

He looked around, his eyes like fire.

"What the hell are you doing?" he shouted.

Andrei looked at him as Viktor led his team inside, killing everyone they came across.

"What we need is to gain access to this building. What did you think? That we'd all sit down over a nice cup of tea? Please, Donald, keep up," Andrei said, walking off toward the house.

There was nothing he could do but follow.

As he walked up the concrete steps to the front doors, he could clearly see the devastation the Russian terrorists had wrought. Dead bodies littered the hallway, callously gunned down before they had a chance to retaliate.

He quickly stepped over the body of Watson and followed the others inside.

By the time he was standing in the hallway, Viktor was returning from clearing the interior from further threats.

"All clear," the burly Russian said.

Bainbridge did a quick mental tally—twelve dead bodies. He had to admit, they were ruthlessly efficient.

"Make sure there will be no surprises. I want the surveillance cameras online. Tell me the instant the Prime Minister enters the driveway," Andrei said to Sergei.

Bainbridge looked back through the open doors to the outside.

Come on, Jack, don't let this happen, he thought as he watched the doors close, locking him inside.

CHAPTER THIRTY-THREE

Prime Minister Andrew Chambers sat in the rear of the comfortable Jaguar, his thoughts racing. His country was in turmoil, and the Security Services seemed at a loss to prevent further loss of life.

The man he trusted to run his private army, as it was known, had been suspicious in his absence. He had been relieved to hear his voice when he had finally got hold of him. If anyone had a solution to this menace, it would be him.

He was beginning to realize he had been relying too heavily on Bainbridge and his SI6 organization, something he decided to rectify once this meeting was over. In the past, a small group of elite individuals had been able to pull off remarkable results, but recently, their lack of manpower and size had led to this incident. They just had not been able to contain this threat. Perhaps it was time to incorporate them into a larger group, such as MI6, or disband them altogether. He would know what to do once this meeting had been held.

As he looked through the front windscreen, he saw

the safe house driveway as his driver steered towards the entrance.

As they drove up towards it, he hoped Bainbridge had some very brilliant ideas to end this, or it would be the end of his career.

"He's coming, just like you said," Sergei said as he looked up from the monitor screen.

Andrei turned to Bainbridge, "Get ready to greet him."

Bainbridge had been waiting for this moment, hoping his men had figured out the Hierarchy's plan.

Viktor had his men arranged around the entrance to the safe house in preparation for the Prime Minister's arrival. If the PM heeded his words and arrived alone with just a small detail, then they would easily be overpowered, and there was nothing he could do to warn them.

Something still bothered him about his last conversation with Andrei though. There was something he said, whether it was a slip or not, he had picked up on it. While waiting for this moment, his mind had desperately tried to work through all the possibilities of that one remark.

He thought he'd figured out their plan, but according to Andrei, he'd figured out most of it, but not all.

What had he missed?

Would he have time to figure it all out before the PM arrived? More importantly, could he do anything about it if he did?

He would soon know as the PM's car pulled up in front of the house.

"Okay, Tony, you know what to do," Jack said through his comm.

"Copy that," Tony replied.

"I have eyes on the PM's vehicle. As soon as he gets out, we move in," Jack said.

Jack set his jaw in grim determination. This was the final act in a play he'd been an unwilling participant in, and all that was about to change as Chambers got out of the car.

———

The door opened, and Bainbridge stood there, ready to greet the Prime Minister.

"Prime Minister, you came," he said as he saw him walking towards him. This comment startled the Prime Minister, which it was meant to. He wanted to alert him without actually coming out and saying so. He saw the reaction in Chamber's eyes, the reaction he wanted. He hoped he would get back in the car and drive off, but it didn't happen.

Slowly he shook his head carefully in the hope that he would get the message.

"Is there something wrong, Donald?" Chambers asked, stopping momentarily.

Before Bainbridge could react, Andrei pushed past him, gun extended, "No, Prime Minister, not for us anyway," he said, and he pulled the trigger.

———

Jack saw Chambers walk towards the doorway and made his move.

Running across the car park, he angled his approach so he could see into the entrance.

He saw Bainbridge standing there with a strange look on his face, then, as the Prime Minister paused, he saw another larger figure push past with a gun aimed at the PM.

In a flash, he aimed and fired his Walther a split second before the newcomer fired his own weapon. He knew he had little hope of hitting his target, he was running, and the angle was difficult, but it still had the desired effect.

Within seconds, he had reached the terrified Prime Minister, who was cowering by his car as his guards attempted to cover him by firing into the doorway.

Jack grabbed Chambers by the arm, hauling him around the back of the vehicle he had arrived in to safety.

"What the fuck is going on here?" he shouted over the sound of gunfire.

"An attempt on your life, sir, to discredit the security services in general and SI6 in particular," Jack said, waving the PM to silence. "Stay here and allow us to do our jobs, sir."

Moving off to the side to get a better shot, he touched his earbud, "Tony, where the hell are you?"

"Coming up now on your flank," Tony's voice came through loud and clear.

"We were too late, damn it, they've closed the door," Jack grumbled.

"We're going to have to breach it and fast," Tony said.

Jack agreed but silently thought their chances were slim to none. How the hell were they supposed to get Bainbridge out now?

CHAPTER THIRTY-FOUR

Bainbridge managed to throw off Andrei's aim by ramming his shoulder into him as he fired.

"What the fuck!" the Russian exclaimed, anger contorting his features.

Gunshots peppered the doorframe, and he saw his captor back up into the hallway as bullets narrowly missed his head.

The door was quickly slammed shut, and Andrei turned on him, his pistol aimed right at him.

"What're you going to do, Andrei? Kill me? You said you needed me," he said, staring the man straight in the eye.

"Not anymore," Andrei said and pulled the trigger. The bullet struck Bainbridge in the center of his forehead, smashing through his skull and painting the floor behind him with his blood. The shock of the shot forced his eyes open wide. His mouth worked as his dying mind tried to form words his mouth would never utter. Finally, he keeled over, falling heavily to the floor, dead.

"Sergei, pull the hard drive from the security cameras, we're leaving," he shouted.

To Viktor, he said, "We need a diversion so we can leave, get to work."

Viktor simply nodded, then moved off to marshal his men.

He glanced at Bainbridge's body, "That was for my brother. The rest of your men will pay the same price."

Without a second glance, he turned and walked off.

———

Outside the building, Jack heard the sound that lifted his spirits.

The chopper came in to hover over the safe house, and zip lines were thrown out of the open door. Swiftly bodies clad in dark combat fatigues came rushing down to the ground. Commander Dark had arrived with reinforcements, his men from 'C' Squadron of the Special Boat Service.

"About fucking time," he muttered with a hint of a smile. He fancied their chances now they had backup worth a damn.

"Okay, Tony, move in now," he said as the SBS men landed and immediately went into formation, ready to move in.

Things were about to get interesting.

———

Commander Dark was the first one out of the chopper, leading his men down to the ground.

He had made the call requesting their assistance, and

his CO had complied without hesitation, considering what was at stake.

His comms were synched to those Jack and Tony were using, so they were all on the same channel.

"On your command, Jack, it's your call," he said as he and his team of three positioned themselves, ready to move.

"Breach, breach, breach," Jack said, giving the command to enter the building.

One of the SBS men approached the entrance and placed a small package on the door. This was an explosive device specifically designed so that the force of the explosion would be directed toward the door, blowing it open. He retreated quickly around the side of the building as his partner watched, ready to detonate as soon as he was clear.

The charge went off, blowing the huge door clean off its hinges and sending it flying into the hallway.

The four SBS men rushed through the opening, weapons up and ready to fire at anything that moved.

John saw Viktor first as he was positioned by the staircase, using it for cover. A quick burst from his MP5 sent him spinning to the ground as bullets stitched a path across his torso.

Gunfire erupted around him as the other members of his team took out the remaining hostiles.

In seconds, the safe house had been breached. Shouts of "Clear" from his team informed John that the building was safe to enter.

Jack and Tony rushed into the hallway, looking for their boss.

"He's over there," John said. He'd spotted Bainbridge's body on entering.

He locked eyes with Jack as Tony rushed to the side of his boss and friend of many years. That one glance conveyed to Jack all he needed to know. John had seen enough bodies in his career with the SBS to know that Bainbridge was indeed dead.

"I'm sorry, Jack, he was like that when we breached," he said as Jack went to stand by him, unable yet to tear his eyes from the body.

John could see the pain etched across Jack's face, the pain of grief and failure.

"Where are they?" Jack asked.

John was about to answer when one of his team came back, "Sir, it looks like they exited through the back, but that's not all, sir," he said, the words tumbling out in a rush.

Both Jack and John looked at the soldier.

"Go on," John urged.

"It looks like they took the hard drive to the surveillance cameras, sir. Whatever happened in here, they have it."

"Why would they take that?" John mused.

He saw Jack's expression change as realization dawned. "They can alter whatever happened here to make it appear however they want."

"Why, what did happen before we got here?" John asked.

"Bainbridge was in the door to greet the PM as he arrived. They tried to shoot him. I think they are going to implicate Bainbridge and SI6 in all of this. I think it was their plan to assassinate Chambers and pin it on Bainbridge, that's why they kept him alive so long. They needed him to communicate with the PM after the attacks so he could lure him here and then kill him, making it look like it was all SI6's fault. When their attempt failed, they no longer had any use for him, so they shot him. They now have the security camera's feed, and they can alter it to suit their needs."

John looked at him as what he said sank in.

"This isn't over yet."

CHAPTER THIRTY-FIVE

Jack and Tony returned to SI6 HQ to contemplate what to do next.

"What do we do now, Tony?" Jack asked.

The drive back had been completed in total silence as Jack allowed his friend to deal with the loss of his friend in his own way. He knew they had been friends for years, even before Bainbridge took over the mantle of head of SI6, so this was particularly hard for him. It was almost like losing a member of his family, something Jack could relate to.

Tony looked at him, his eyes blank. When he spoke, he sounded like a man defeated.

"I have no idea," he said softly.

Jack knew what he was going through; he had been struck by the same shock of grief not so long ago. He also knew Tony would bounce back and recover, it would just take time though. Time they didn't have, unfortunately. The Hierarchy were still out there with the footage from the safe house, and God only knew what they planned on doing with it.

The only thing in their favor was that they had saved the life of the Prime Minister. They had explained the Hierarchy had lured him to the safe house so they could kill him and implicate Bainbridge and SI6. He had seemed to understand and had been grateful for the intervention that had prevented the plan coming to fruition. How long that gratitude would last though, was anyone's guess.

"Is it true Bainbridge is dead?" Deakin asked as he rushed into the room.

"I'm afraid so, Robert. We were too late to save him," explained Jack as Tony paraded around the room.

"What're you going to do? They can't get away with this, you have to do something."

"At the moment, I have no idea what we can do," Tony said as he sat down heavily in the chair behind the desk.

Jack heard footsteps approaching and turned to see a dark-suited man followed by two others, clearly security, enter the room as if they owned the place.

"Just who the hell are you?" Jack demanded.

"Simon Bennett, Deputy Director of MI6," the dark-suited man said, eyeing everyone in the room as if gauging them. Jack thought he had the look of a predator who seemed to be stalking his prey.

"Ordinarily, this meeting would take place in my office in Westminster, but due to the severity of the situation and the urgency of it, I thought it best to conduct it here before you did something more rash than normal," Bennett said.

"What do you want?" Tony asked without preamble.

"I'm shutting you down," Bennett said, looking straight at Tony.

"You're doing what?" exploded Jack, stalking straight

up to the slim figure of the man from the security services.

The two security men stared Jack down as they stood at Bennett's shoulders.

"I'm shutting you down, you heard me the first time, Cross. I've been in talks with the Prime Minister since he returned from your so-called safe house where he almost lost his life, and it's been decided that we take action before this gets leaked to the press."

"I get it, you're throwing us to the wolves now so that when this does get out, you can say you took the necessary action as soon as you were made aware of it," Tony said.

"Come on now, Armstrong. You can't have even imagined there wouldn't be a price to pay for what's just happened, can you?"

"So what happens now?" Jack asked. He couldn't believe this was actually happening.

"Simple, SI6 will be absorbed into MI6 so that their actions can be governed and controlled."

"When you say 'absorbed', you mean it won't exist anymore, don't you?"

"Not for you, Cross, your services will no longer be required."

"You're firing me?"

"Look at it as an early retirement with benefits. You'll receive a full pension, and you can have the time to grieve properly over the loss of your family. The rest of you will be assigned different duties; it's for the best, gentlemen."

"When do the new orders take effect?" Tony asked.

"With immediate effect. I want all SI6 files to be sent over a secure channel to MI6 HQ. Once that has successfully been done, then we can close this place down,"

Bennett said, turning and leaving the room with his two guards.

"How long will that take, Robert?" Jack asked the IT guy.

"It can be done in a couple of minutes, sir," Deakin replied nervously, looking from Jack to Tony.

"No, it'll take a lot longer than that, surely. You'll have to locate them, go through them all to ensure they're all there, then bundle them into a data package before sending them off. Could take days," Jack said. Deakin smiled when he realized what he was up to.

"Weeks, maybe," he agreed.

"In the meantime, you can locate me those responsible for Bainbridge's death. I want you to check the CCTV cameras leading up to the safe house and see if you can get an image of whoever was in the cars that took Bainbridge there. Once you have an image, run it through facial recognition to find out who they are, then do a search for the bastards. I want to know where they are now. Until MI6 get those files, SI6 still exists, and we're going to use that time to find and kill those responsible for all this."

CHAPTER THIRTY-SIX

Andrei sat down in the plush leather seat of the Gulfstream G550 and looked out of the small window at the tarmac below.

"How long before we can take off?" he asked Sergei, who sat across from him.

"I instructed the pilot you'd want to leave as soon as we boarded. He assured me that the flight plan has been logged and we're just awaiting our slot. It shouldn't be long," the smaller man said as he opened his ever-present laptop.

"Okay, Deakin, what have you got for me?" Tony asked as he entered Deakin's room. Jack and the Commander were in tow behind, all of them anxious for some news.

"It's as we thought, sir. Andrei Petrov and his comrade Sergei Ivanovich were responsible for kidnapping Bainbridge. I have them arriving at the safe house and leaving via another route after the gun battle with our boys. I tracked their movements through various other CCTV cameras around the city, and I found them at a small, private airfield climbing aboard a Gulfstream G550," Deakin told them, not turning around to look at them. He was busy with his computer, his fingers flying over the keyboard as he input commands.

"Where the fuck are they going?" Jack asked, forcing past Tony to stand over the small IT guy.

"I'm working on that now," he said, feverishly typing away. "Crete, they're going to Crete," he said finally.

Jack took a step back and looked at Tony.

"They're going back to where this all began. He's going to take control of the Mafia contingent on the island and bring them under the Hierarchy's rule," Tony said.

"We can't let that happen," Jack stated.

Tony looked at Commander Dark and then at Jack. "Okay, let's do this before MI6 shuts us down for good. Let's make Bainbridge's death stand for something."

"Copy that," Dark said without hesitation.

"I'm in," agreed Jack.

"Inform Fairfax that we're on our way and tell them to log a flight plan to Crete ASAP, and Robert," Tony paused while Deakin turned to look at him, "cover your tracks. I don't want MI6 finding out what we're doing here, okay?"

"Certainly, sir, like they could anyway," Deakin said with an arrogant smirk.

Overlooking his remark, Tony turned to the others, "Right, let's do this, SI6's last mission. We have the Hierarchy in our crosshairs, time to pull the trigger."

Simon Bennett was waiting to enter the Prime Minister's office in Ten Downing Street. He had been summoned there upon his return to MI6 HQ from his meeting with the remaining staff of SI6.

He had a feeling about what the summons was about and had prepared for it.

The door opened, and the PM's aide appeared, holding it open.

You may go in now, the Prime Minister will see you," he said effetely.

With a slight nod, Bennett got up from his seat and walked past the slim aide.

"Come in, Simon, take a seat. So glad you could make it," Chambers said as Bennett entered the room. The aide exited once he was sure he was in, closing the door behind him.

"I got the impression it was urgent, so I came right away, sir," Bennett said as he took the offered seat opposite him.

"Where are we on the Hierarchy situation?"

"Excuse me, I'm not sure I understand, sir," Bennett replied, a little flustered but remaining cool to the eye.

"What is the situation regarding the Hierarchy?" Chambers said, spearing Bennett under his steely gaze.

"No disrespect, sir, but that's the same question worded a little differently, and I already answered it."

"Not to my satisfaction, you didn't, hence my asking again."

Bennett sat back and returned Chambers' gaze.

"I have taken steps to incorporate the files gathered by SI6 into MI6. From the data held inside those files, I hope to be able to learn enough about this organization to be able to form a plan against it," Bennett said guardedly.

"Explain exactly what you mean by incorporate the files from SI6," Chambers said, keeping him fixed in his steely gaze.

"I have shut down SI6 and ordered them to pass over everything they have to me."

"Bennett, this is not about you. This is about doing what's right for the country, and if you are unable or unwilling to see that plain fact, then I will have you removed from your post immediately. Is that clear?"

Bennett swallowed as he kept his cool. He had allowed his jealousy of SI6 and their result record to fuel his ambition and had made his move too soon.

"Perfectly, sir," he said softly.

"I can tell you firsthand that the Hierarchy presents a clear and present danger to this nation, and it is up to you and your department to do something about it. I would think you would be embracing SI6, their knowledge, and expertise in this regard to help you in this endeavor, and yet here you are, telling me you have shut them down. What were you thinking, man? You may have destroyed our best chance of success in this situation. I want you to get out of here and go and rectify this now. Do I make myself perfectly clear?"

"Sir, I would just like to say that you might think I screwed up here, but what I have done is to protect the country and this Government. I have given you plausible deniability. What you have no knowledge of cannot hurt you or this Government. That's what I've been doing, sir. There is no reason for you to know any of the details. In fact, knowing this much can jeopardize the outcome, so with respect, I will say nothing more."

"Forgive me if I misjudged you, Bennett, these recent events have rattled everyone, but not you, it seems. I'm amazed at how you kept a cool head in all of this, and I take back my earlier comments. Please continue, and this meeting never took place."

"Oh, this meeting took place, sir. We just talked about something else. You invited me to ask about the progress I was making with SI6, who are responsible for some of the events recently. I, of course, informed you that I had taken steps to shut that operation down. That is all, sir."

Bennett got to his feet calmly and left the room, closing the door behind him. He had his phone out and was making the call as he left.

"Are the SI6 people still at their HQ?" he asked as he headed for the car. When he got word that they had left, he smiled. He knew they would, he had left them no choice really.

"Keep me informed of their movements," he said. He put his phone away before the person on the other end had finished speaking.

As he climbed into the back seat of his staff car, he relaxed a little. If things went the way he predicted, then all this would be over soon, and the job of rebuilding could begin, not only repairing the damage done to the city, but to the reputation of the security services and SI6 in particular.

He grabbed his phone the instant it rang, putting it straight to his ear. "Are they on their way to Crete?"

"They went to Fairfax, sir, where they took their Gulfstream. They're headed for Heraklion International as we speak," the voice said in his ear.

"Good work, keep me informed."

To the driver, he said, "Take me back to the office."

CHAPTER THIRTY-SEVEN

The trio of operatives had arrived at Fairfield and, like Bennett had been told, boarded the Gulfstream that was waiting for them.

As they took off, Jack realized how tired he was. They had all been running on adrenaline all day with little chance of rest or eating anything. He stretched and surrendered to a yawn he had been battling against. When he finished, he saw Tony looking at him.

"I think our first priority when we land is for us all to grab a few hours of sleep. We can meet up again over breakfast to organize our plan. I'll have Deakin monitor Petrov to keep tabs on his movements so we know where he'll be," Tony said.

"You won't get any arguments from me, I'm knackered," Jack said through another massive yawn.

Dark said, "If that's the plan, then I'm catching some Z's now while we have the chance, just in case we have to hit the ground running." He turned toward the side of the plane, rested his head against his arm, and within seconds, was fast asleep.

Jack saw this and followed suit, saying, "Me too," leaving Tony on his own.

"Fuck it, when in Rome..." he said, and within seconds, he too was asleep.

The entire flight, they slept as soundly as they could've hoped for. The only sound apart from the hum of the engines were the murmurs from Jack as he dreamt the same dream that had haunted him since he had watched his wife and daughter brutally slain before his very eyes. Tonight though, exhaustion kept the dreams at bay for a time at least, allowing him the rest he very much needed.

Bennett was sitting in his office in MI6 HQ, thinking about the three men he had manipulated.

He had the interests of the country at heart, and big decisions like this one, where lives were put in the firing line, were part of the job. If he couldn't assign people to do the dangerous tasks for the greater good, then he had no business being in this trade.

Fortunately for him, not for others, he was very good at what he did. That wasn't to say he didn't have a conscience. On the contrary, his conscience was extremely active, but he was exceptionally good at compartmentalizing. If something had to be done and there was no other way, he would make that decision and worry about the consequences to him later, the job must always come first.

In some respects, that was the reason he was still a bachelor. He could not put someone else through what he had to face on a daily basis, and his conscience would not allow him to keep secrets from someone he shared his life with. Luckily he had never met anyone to challenge that belief, at least not yet.

He had fired Jack Cross on the spot. He was well aware of what the man had gone through, and it was a testament to his testicular fortitude that he was still operating. He was probably focused on the task at hand only because it had ties to his dead family. Once he severed that tie, he would need time to grieve, his decision would give him that time.

Colonel Armstrong would be an asset to MI6 at any stage of his career, but he had bigger plans ahead for him, which just left Commander Dark. He could return to his role of commander of 'C' Squadron in the SBS without as much as a hiccup.

To the general public, the events would be over with and the perpetrators brought to justice, killed in a gun battle with the authorities. To the Intelligence community, SI6 would be shut down, and that rogue operation ended. In reality, it would be something else entirely. Something would rise from the ashes here, something exceptional, but for it to succeed, those three needed to survive.

Andrei's plane landed after a four-hour, uneventful flight.

He rose from his seat, refreshed from his sleep, and moved to exit the plane.

As he stepped onto the steps, he looked around Heraklion International Airport and took a deep breath savoring the warm, fragrant air. He walked down the steps onto the tarmac, followed by Sergei.

"Is everything in place?" Andrei asked.

"I've made the calls as you instructed. They'll be

there, you don't have to worry," Sergei replied, placing a comforting hand on his shoulder.

Andrei turned on him, his eyes blazing as he shrugged the hand free. "You think I'm worried? I'm not worried. I'm furious. We failed to destroy all of SI6. We may have destroyed their ability to organize, but those responsible for my brother's death are still alive. This will not stand with the Hierarchy. To them, failure is not an option. To me, because they still live, I will not rest until their blood is on my hands."

Sergei stepped back from the onslaught of his anger. Carefully he said, "I've been monitoring signals from MI6. They have shut down all SI6 operations, but Cross, Armstrong, and one other boarded an unscheduled flight at that small airfield they use and are headed here. They arrive shortly, you'll get your chance for revenge, Andrei."

"Just those three, eh!"

"That's all that's left of SI6."

"Well, they won't last long, I'll see to that. Make the preparations then, let's get to the hotel."

Sergei breathed a little easier as he saw his friend walk towards the waiting car. He took out his phone and made the call as instructed before following him into the car.

CHAPTER THIRTY-EIGHT

"They're here," Jack said as he saw the other Gulfstream parked across the airport.

They had arrived at Heraklion Airport as night had closed in on the island. It was still very warm, and as he walked across the tarmac to the Arrivals section, he felt the warmth soothe his tired body.

"Well, there's not a lot we can do tonight. I suggest we find a hotel for the night, get a hot meal inside us then we can confer with Deakin in the morning about what we intend to do next. By then, I hope he'll know a bit more about where they are and what they might be planning," Tony said as he fell in step with him and Dark.

All three of them were carrying their go-bags, which held everything they would need for the trip.

"Can I just say, if you intend on planning an assault on them, we are going to need way more weaponry than we have with us, which is nothing seeing as how you insisted on us landing here instead of the military base like I suggested," Dark said grumpily.

"If we had landed at the military base, MI6 would

know exactly where we were and could've called ahead for them to detain us. At least here, they have no authority to call ahead, unless they put us on a terrorist watch list, which has just occurred to me," Tony explained. "That shows we all need rest, none of us are thinking clearly enough. Let's hope they didn't put us on that list I just mentioned, or we'll never get any further than the arrivals lounge."

"That won't happen," Jack stated confidently.

This brought a stare from Tony and a question, "How can you be so sure?"

"Plausible deniability, they want the Hierarchy stopped for what happened in London. Andrei has planned all this and for the blame to land squarely on our shoulders, to show just how incompetent we are in being unable to prevent these attacks. He also planned to have us die back there as the final act in this play he produced. The Government want this to end, so they shut us down, knowing full well we wouldn't let Bainbridge's death go unpunished. Bennett knew we would take action, and in shutting us down, he's protected the Government. If we succeed, then he can take credit for a covert operation well planned and orchestrated by MI6, if not, we will take the blame as rogue operators that the Government knew nothing about and had no control over."

"The devious bastard," commented Dark.

"He's just doing his job, that's all," Jack said.

Tony agreed, "I've seen similar things happen before, this is nothing unusual."

"I don't blame him, any of us would probably do just the same if we were in his place, and I'm just glad I'm not. I'd much rather be out here in the firing line, at least here, you know where you stand," Jack said.

"Well, if Bennett has his say, you won't be for much longer," Tony said.

"Will any of us?" Dark asked.

That was a sobering thought and brought them all to silence whilst they strode through to the Arrivals hall.

Bennett finished up at the office and then went home for the evening. He picked up a 'meal for one' at his local Tesco Extra, then went straight home to his apartment overlooking the River Thames.

The ride home had been serene and routine. He spoke to no one, and no one bothered him, the quirk of living in a huge city and feeling totally alone. It never bothered him; in fact, it bothered him more if someone attempted to strike up a conversation as he preferred to make this journey in silence.

When he was preparing his evening meal, he found himself ruminating over the SI6 operatives and what they may be facing in Crete.

Picking up the phone, he decided to make a call that would help them should they need it. He had an asset on the island, an operative who had just finished off a mission. They wouldn't like the new orders, but it was a necessary part of the job. No one at work knew of this asset, and he wanted to keep it that way. It was his ace in the hole and was brought out to play only on the rarest of occasions, this being one of them.

He waited, uncertain if the call would be answered, and when it was, a smile crossed his lips, and he began to speak.

Craig Vaughn was sitting at his table in the restaurant, about to start his evening meal, when his phone rang.

"Yes?" he said. He had recognized the number and knew who the caller was. The phone had a special chip that encoded certain calls, scrambled them, making them untraceable and jammed if anyone was trying to listen in.

"There is an unsanctioned operation on Crete which might need an oversight. Can you help out with that?" Bennett asked.

"Send me all the details and I'll take a look. Once I've reviewed the file, I'll inform you of my decision, and you can make the usual payment," Vaughn replied.

"I've just sent the file to your phone. I'll expect your decision in the morning," Bennett said, ending the call.

Vaughn looked at his phone and accessed the file he'd just received. He began to eat his meal as he read the file.

He was intrigued by what he read. The attacks on London, the kidnapping of Bainbridge, all just to implicate SI6 and make them look incompetent, was a brilliant plan. The three operatives who had come to Crete after Andrei Petrov were definitely up against a formidable enemy. The odds were against them, that much was true. Should he get involved though? That was the question he had to ask himself.

He put away his phone to concentrate on his dinner. The Stifado really was quite excellent, the meat rich and tender, and the sauce was out of this world. He finished off the meal and sat back, thinking.

Even though he had just finished a job for Bennett, he found himself drawn to this one. His last op had been a simple surveillance job, no danger in that one. He had told Bennett he didn't want any more jobs that would see him putting himself at risk, those days were long since past. Yet he found himself thinking of a plan to help these guys without letting them know he was even there. He was a ghost, and that's how he liked it. He worked best from the shadows.

Picking up his phone, he returned the call. "Okay, I'll take the job. Send the fee through the usual channels, I'll commence when the transfer has been completed," he said, putting his phone away. There was no need for him to hear what Bennett said, he knew his terms would be met.

Getting to his feet, he left a few euros on the table, enough to cover his meal and a good tip, then left the restaurant and headed for his room.

When he woke the next morning, he would be working again.

CHAPTER THIRTY-NINE

Andrei woke in the comfortable bed of his hotel room. His sleep had refreshed him, but he still felt anger at not being able to fulfill his mission to his satisfaction.

That was about to change though. The ones he had wanted to kill for the death of his brother were within his grasp. They had wandered into his domain like a fly into a spider's web. Whether knowingly or unknowingly, it didn't matter, the outcome would be the same; they would die by his hand.

The sun was streaming through the window, and he felt its warmth already, even this early in the morning. He climbed out of bed and walked naked into the bathroom to take a shower.

As the water helped revive him, he began to formulate a plan that would crush those that followed him here. First, he had to visit the local Mafia boss and let him know his days of being in power were at an end.

He quickly dressed in a thin cotton shirt and cargo shorts; finally, he stepped into leather sandals and left his room. He would meet Sergei for breakfast as arranged the night before, and he would relay his orders.

As he entered the restaurant, his spirits were lifting as he looked out over the sea view. He decided to relax on the beach later and top up his tan, but first, he had business to attend to.

———

Jack took a sip of his coffee as he looked out over the balcony of his room. The view of the Aegean was breathtaking, the early morning sun glinting off the azure waters as they lapped up against the shore.

He had woken early, showered, then dressed in a shirt and shorts before making himself a pot of coffee. As he drank, his thoughts returned to recent events, as they usually did in the quiet moments. In particular, the death of his wife and daughter, watching that happen in front of him was something he knew he would never be able to reconcile with. The Hierarchy had been behind it, but in some respects, he felt some of the blame must land squarely on his shoulders. If he had chosen to agree with his wife when she had pleaded with him not to go on that last mission, they would still be alive today. Had he not become involved, Alex Berg, the Hierarchy hit man, would not have trailed him to his home in an attempt to exact revenge for his interfering in their plot. They would not have fought, and his wife and daughter would not have been killed because of all that.

The intelligent side of his brain knew this was a falsehood. Berg's choice to attack him was his alone, and it was his choice to shoot an innocent woman and child, but the emotional and logical side of his brain made him feel responsible because their deaths were a direct consequence of his actions.

This was a burden he was going to take to the grave with him, and all he could do was learn to cope. The grief and guilt would remain with him like a scar on his soul.

He hadn't had time to dwell on this because of the Hierarchy attacking SI6 HQ and all the other attacks in and around London, but now, in the quiet of the still morning air, it all came back to haunt him once more.

Darkness threatened to overwhelm him until his phone rang, momentarily breaking him free from his painful reverie.

"Yes, Tony?" he said when he recognized the caller. He hoped his voice didn't betray his emotional state as he tried to sound calm.

"We're meeting down in the restaurant for breakfast," Tony said.

"Copy that, on my way," he replied. Lifting his mug to his lips, he thought about his wife and daughter one more time. "Miss you two. I'll see you soon, but not today," he said, wiping a solitary tear from his eye as he turned to leave the balcony. Work summoned, and he had to answer. It was all he had left.

Vaughn was up just after dawn, making preparations.

He breakfasted early after a quick shower, then sat down with his laptop at the table in his room. He hacked into the satellite overhead and then used that to hack into the airport CCTV cameras. It didn't take him long before he had everything he needed. Once he had images of those he was looking for, he ran their faces through the facial recognition software installed on his laptop.

The images ran on the program he had developed for just such an occasion, and it didn't take long before he had a log of every movement of every player in this game since their arrival on the island. He knew where they all were, and what's more, he knew where they were all going. All he had to do was get there first.

CHAPTER FORTY

Andrei sat in the front seat of the silver Mercedes as it pulled up on the road approaching Agios Nicolaos overlooking Mirabello Bay.

In the distance, he could see the yacht at anchor out in the bay, a sleek hundred-and-thirty-footer, in brilliant white with a sharp prow and elegant lines. Moored at the end of the jetty was the small motor launch along with the floatplane, a de Havilland Otter.

This was the home of the local Mafia boss, who had taken over the cell after the death of his brother. He was there to relinquish the new boss of his control and return it to the Hierarchy.

"Okay, Sergei, let's go say hello," he said, urging him to drive on.

As instructed, Sergei drove the Mercedes down the bank towards the harbor. As soon as they pulled up, Andrei was out and stood by the car. He noticed several pairs of eyes had followed them to that point, and one man made his way from the small group of onlookers to stand in front of him.

Andrei sized him up; he was a big man, at least six two, with strong features and dark staring eyes.

"If I were you, I would get back in your car and drive off before you get hurt," he said, his voice gravelly from too many cigarettes.

"You're not me."

He glanced across at Sergei, who had exited the car and come around to stand next to him.

With a nod of his head, Andrei indicated they move off in the direction of the shoreline. As he moved, their reception committee placed a hand on his chest to stop him.

Andrei looked down at the hand, then up into the smirking face of his blockade.

"You have three seconds to remove your hand before I remove it for you," warned Andrei, which elicited a grin from Sergei, he knew what his friend was capable of.

As expected, the big man called his bluff.

Andrei grabbed the wrist in a grip resembling a vice. He removed the hand effortlessly, twisting, applying pressure with his thumb over the pinkie knuckle, which forced the hand into a painful position that the big man had no defense against. In seconds Andrei had him going down onto his knees, a painful grimace twisting his face. To hammer home his point, Andrei smashed the thug in the face with a fist that felt like he'd been hit with a sledgehammer. The thug went down on his back; blood spread across his face from his smashed nose and shattered teeth.

Andrei looked up at the startled group with a challenging stare. No one took up the challenge though, none of them wanted to suffer the same fate as their friend.

"Cowards," Andrei muttered as he turned away and

walked towards the jetty where the motor launch was tied up.

Sergei had a broad smile on his face as he looked at the group. It slipped slightly as his friend walked off. He had been so wrapped up in watching their discomfort at having one of their own having his ass handed to him in front of them that he almost missed Andrei leaving.

Andrei reached the jetty first and was met by two men who were standing by the tethered boat.

"Take me across to that yacht, now," he ordered.

The two men exchanged amused glances before looking back at the stern-faced Russian standing on the dock. Their smiles vanished when they saw the pistol in his hand.

"Was I not clear?" he asked.

The two men parted to allow him on board, followed by Sergei, then they went about releasing the ties and starting up the engine. Andrei knew they would comply, they were low on the ranks of the Mafia and used to following orders.

He and Sergei sat at the rear of the boat as the two men piloted it out into the bay, heading out to the yacht. He had to squint as the sun glistened off the azure waters of the Aegean Sea. With one hand holding his pistol on the two men, he reached for a pair of Ray-Bans and placed them on his face, enabling him to see much better.

As they got closer to the yacht, he could see it much clearer. The wood paneling, the gold fittings all pointed to one thing, wealth. Obviously, the Mafia, since the death of his brother, had attempted to regain control of the area by pouring in sufficient funds to finance an operation of this size.

More details became apparent the closer they got,

including the armed guards patrolling the rear deck where they were heading.

The two pilots' attitude changed the nearer to the yacht they got, and as they pulled up to the ladder at the rear of the impressive boat, they stopped the engines and turned to look at him and Sergei, leaning against the steering controls with their arms crossed, smiling confidently.

"They think they've delivered us into the Lion's Den," he whispered to Sergei.

"Looking at all those guns, I'm wondering if they just might be right. You have this, don't you?" Sergei wondered in the same tone.

"Doubt does not suit you, my friend. I'm a little annoyed you even have to ask," Andrei glanced at him, his brows pinched. He saw in Sergei's eyes that he knew not to piss him off with questions like that.

"I'm sorry, I don't know what came over me," Sergei quickly admonished himself.

"That's more like it. You know me, know what I'm capable of, let's go show them," he said with a nod towards the guards hovering at the railing looking down at them.

He saw their air of confidence born out of having nothing more than local businesses to deal with, something that would play to his benefit.

He saw their attitude toward him alter when they spotted the gun he was holding. They aimed their assault rifles down at him, which was the moment he made his move.

CHAPTER FORTY-ONE

Jack and the others had driven up to the same spot Andrei had arrived at earlier. They had found this area after contacting Deakin back in the UK. He had told them where the local Mafia was based on the island.

Tony had been a little surprised that Bennett had left Robert alone long enough for him to help them out.

"Another bay, another yacht, where do they get their money from?" Jack said when he saw the yacht.

"You make it sound like you do this every other day," Dark commented from the back seat.

"Some days that's just how it feels. In this case, Mike Flynn and I blew up a yacht, not too dissimilar to that one, in this very harbor not too long ago. It's what started all this with the Hierarchy. I'm looking forward to paying those bastards back for what they did."

"Just remember why we're here, Jack, don't make this personal," Tony warned.

"I'm not, they made it personal the moment they attacked and killed my wife and daughter. They started it, all I'm doing is finishing it," Jack snarled.

"Okay, now we've got that out of the way, what's the plan, guys?" Dark interrupted before this got out of hand.

Tony said, "Like you said earlier, Commander, we're going to need some firepower."

"I hear that," Jack agreed.

"Good thing I know a guy then," Tony said with a sly smile. He started the car again and started to drive off.

"Wait, where're we goin'?" Jack asked as they started moving.

"They're not going anywhere, and we need to be somewhere we can pick up everything we need," Tony said as he steered the car along the perilously narrow mountain track.

As Dark sat back, he said, "Well, I, for one, am not venturing down there without at least a couple of guns, maybe a rifle or two, throw in a couple of grenades. I mean, don't literally throw them in, but you get the gist."

"Yeah, we get the gist," Jack said.

———

Vaughn had been watching it all go down from a vantage point sitting in a café near the harbor.

He had been there early, at first having a leisurely breakfast, then just sat reading the morning newspaper and taking in the view of the harbor, which was nothing more than a wooden jetty that ran across the small secluded beach and out into the water.

He gave the impression of not being in the slightest bit interested in what was going on. Apart from a single glance at the slight altercation with the group, which all the customers at the café watched, he kept on reading his newspaper.

From his seat out in the open air at the side of the

café, he had an unobstructed view of the beach and the road the two Russians had used to reach this point. He knew the others would have to use it too, as it was the only way to reach this spot on the island. His peripheral vision was good enough for him to spot traffic moving along the road at the top of the rise.

A car had stopped for a minute or two before moving on. There were many reasons for anyone to do this ranging from holidaymakers enjoying the view to a small trio of agents checking out the lay of the land. He preferred to think it was the latter and would expect to see this particular car again pretty soon.

If the three agents made their move down here or on the yacht, then his job of watching their backs would be more than difficult if he wanted to remain anonymous. He liked this island and had even considered retiring here, but if he had to take an active part in what was to come, then his plans would be thrown through the window. There was no way he would be able to live here as he wanted, not if they knew of his role in the action. He would always be a target for any retribution that would come his way from the Mafia or this new group, the Hierarchy.

He couldn't allow any of this to color his view of what he had to do, he had agreed to this job, and it was too late to back out now, not that he would. He had never accepted a mission and then gone back on his word, and he wasn't about to start now.

He would carry this through, no matter what the outcome, and face the consequences later.

CHAPTER FORTY-TWO

Andrei virtually ran up the ladder at the rear of the yacht, leaving Sergei to watch from the motor launch below.

The two guards watched him come up the ladder with bemused expressions on their faces.

Andrei gambled on them never having faced anyone with enough balls to come up to the yacht and simply climb aboard. It paid off as they backed off a couple of steps, giving him the freedom to jump over the railing.

"Hello guys, is your boss home?" he said, smiling at them as if it was the most natural thing in the world.

The two guards looked at each other, the moment Andrei was waiting for to strike.

Before climbing the ladder, he had replaced his pistol in the waistband of his cargo shorts at the small of his back. The moment they took their eyes off him, he drew the Sig and fired two shots. Each bullet hit its mark, smashing through the skull of each guard, dropping them both. The sound of the gunshots echoed around the bay, alerting the others on board.

Footsteps pounded the deck as more guards came

running to protect the Capo, who Andrei knew was sunning himself on the foredeck.

"Incompetent fools," he muttered as he easily avoided them by walking around the side of the boat. He heard them congregate on the aft deck where he'd been moments before, but by this time, he had almost reached the foredeck. Two armed men faced him, standing in front of the person he had come to see, who was still lounging on a sunbed, seemingly oblivious to the intrusion.

"Freeze!" they shouted, bringing their assault rifles up, ready to fire.

"This can go one of two ways," he said as he aimed his Sig at them both. "You can either put down your weapons, or my sniper will drop you where you stand. It's a difficult shot to be sure. How far would you say it was from the hill over there on the shore, almost three-quarters of a mile, more perhaps? He is good though, he killed his last man from a mile and a half away, so this should be easy enough, don't you think?"

He watched as the guards became jittery, wanting to glance at the shore but afraid any movement would elicit them getting shot. Slowly, and without any word from the seated man, they lowered their weapons to the deck.

This movement made the Capo turn around to see what was going on.

"Who the fuck are you, and what're you doing on my yacht?" he snarled in disgust as his guards sloped off towards the aft section of the boat.

"I'm your new boss, Andrei Petrov."

At the sound of his name, Andrei saw the color drain from the Capo's face.

"I had nothing to do with your brother's death, I swear," he pleaded.

"Oh, if I thought that, you'd be dead already. I know exactly who was responsible, and they are on their way here to try and kill me, but that's for later. Right now, I'm here to issue you with your new orders from the Hierarchy."

The white walls of the villa shone in the bright morning sun as they drove up the driveway.

"Do we need to know where we're going and who we're going to meet?" Jack asked when he saw their destination.

"He's an old friend. I'm sure he'll give us all the help we need," Tony replied.

He slowed the car and pulled it up in front of the villa. The door opened, and someone stormed out, pointing a shotgun at them as they got out.

"You have some balls showing up here after what you did," said the owner of the shotgun furiously. He walked up to Tony, aiming the weapon at his face.

"I ought to blow your head clean off right here, right now," he said. The gun was held rock steady, aimed straight at his face.

Jack's eyes darted from the angry man to Tony, who stood stock still, staring him straight in the eye. If he was afraid, it didn't show.

"Before you do anything you might regret, why don't you just point that gun away while we talk," Jack said, hoping to ease the tension in the air a little.

"Back off, Jack. If he wants to blow my head off, I won't stop him, and neither will any of you."

"Are you crazy?" Jack asked. "The man looks like he's

getting ready to top you, and you don't want us to intervene? I didn't come here to watch any of us die."

"Stand down, soldier. If Papandrou wants to kill me, he has every right. You're right, Papandrou, you have every right to want me dead. It was me who sent Mike Flynn to help out your brother, and because of that, he wound up dead. That's on me, and it's something I have to live with. I have no excuses. What I did, I thought was for the best."

"For the best? You bastard, you got Georgios and Maria killed, and for what? Tell me, Tony, what did you achieve? Did their deaths prove anything, or did they die for nothing?" Papandrou was spitting words out at Tony in uncontrollable rage; it was only through a herculean effort that prevented him from pulling the trigger and killing him.

"That's what we're here to do, to address that imbalance," Tony said.

"You're here to kill someone, but this time, you've come yourself and not left it to your lackey."

"Yes, but we need your help."

Papandrou stepped back and lowered the shotgun slightly. "You need my help to do what?"

"I don't need you to do anything other than supply us with weapons," Tony said.

Papandrou glanced at Jack and Dark.

"Who're these two?"

"I'm the lackey he sent last time," Jack said.

CHAPTER FORTY-THREE

"Nice boat, your business must be booming," Andrei observed as he sat down in one of the chairs near the Capo's lounger.

Behind him stood Sergei, who had found his way on board escorted by the guards who now were showing them both respect.

"All this isn't from merely the exploitation of local businesses, surely?" Andrei said as he made himself comfortable.

"Drugs?" Sergei interrupted.

Andrei glanced over his shoulder, a slight turn of the head, nothing more, giving the impression he was considering his subordinate's suggestion.

"That would make sense, I suppose. The Mafia has always had their hands in the drug trade, and once my brother was gone, they would seize upon the opportunity to regain control of the area. That ends today. The Hierarchy is once more back in control, any problems?" he asked, looking back at the man who was sitting nervously across from him. "I'm sorry, we haven't been properly introduced. You know my name, but who are you?"

"Vasos Manikas," the seated man said.

"How many trips a week do you have to make to pick up your supply, and where from?" Andrei asked.

Manikas leaned forward and said, "It doesn't matter, you won't stop them. You come in here, and you think you can just take over because what, your brother was some big shot in some organization no one has even heard of? The Hierarchy, come on, who the fuck is that? The Cartels and the Mafia are in a partnership over the drugs, and you think you're going to stand in their way with just the two of you. Good luck with that."

Andrei smiled at the man's outburst. It was the first time he'd shown the slightest sign he had any balls. He glanced around at Sergei, who returned his smile and then looked down at the deck.

"Well, you could be right, but you won't be around to see any of it," he said. He drew his pistol and fired. The bullet hit Manikas in the center of his forehead and passed through, spraying the deck with blood and gore. The look of shock in his eyes suddenly altered as the light went out in them as he fell back, dead.

Others came running at the sound of the gunshot. Andrei calmly stood up to face them.

"You have a choice, work for the Hierarchy, or you can join your old boss," he said.

Andrei was not surprised to find they all agreed to join them.

"Why would you think I can get weapons for you?" Papandrou asked.

Tony held up his hands, "I didn't mean you. I just thought you'd know someone who could."

Papandrou looked at all of them as he thought about it.

Nodding, he said, "I may know someone. Wait here while I make a call."

Jack watched him walk off back into the villa and walked up next to Tony.

"Do you think he'll help?" he asked.

"I suppose we'll know soon enough."

"Next time you want to make a half-arsed play like this one, a little warning would be nice," Jack said as he walked off to go and stand next to Dark.

"Be prepared. I don't like this one bit," he said quietly.

"I agree, something's not quite right here," Dark said, confirming his own doubts about the situation.

Andrei sat in the lounger, relaxing as Sergei opened his laptop.

"Can you find out where they are?" he asked, then he heard one of the deck crew approaching. Looking over his shoulder, he saw a man holding a phone.

"What?"

"He says he wants to talk to Vasos, but he's dead, so you'd better deal with this," said the man thrusting the phone at him.

Andrei took the phone and listened. Finally, when the caller stopped speaking, he said, "Bring them here."

As the call had ended, he put the phone down and looked into the expectant face of his friend.

"Don't bother; I know exactly where they are."

Papandrou came back out to them, his face a mask, hiding his real feelings.

"I've made the arrangements, we are to go to them, and you will get everything you want," he said.

Jack looked at the Greek and then back at Dark. Quietly he said, "Eyes open. I've got a feeling something's not quite right here."

"Me too," Dark agreed, and they both got in the car after Tony.

"He says to follow him," Tony said, unconcerned. When he saw the look in their eyes, he asked, "What?"

"Do you trust him?" Jack asked.

"He may be angry and grieving over the loss of his family, but he'll come through for us," he replied.

"Just hope you're right," Jack said.

Tony turned away from their stares and mumbled, "Me too."

They sat quietly while they waited for their escort to get in his car and drive, the air inside their vehicle alive with the tension they felt.

Jack knew Tony was putting a lot of faith in his friend, but he felt it was misguided by the guilt he felt over the death of his friend's brother and daughter. It was a mistake that could cost all of them their lives.

CHAPTER FORTY-FOUR

"Does this road look familiar to you?" Jack asked Dark in the rear seat of their vehicle.

"Yep, we're heading back to Agios Nicolaos."

The vehicle in front of them suddenly pulled up, forcing them to come to a halt behind it.

"What's happening? Why did we stop?" Jack asked, looking around to see if he could see anything.

Tony said, "I'm not sure, it looks like the road is blocked."

"Get out, now," Jack warned.

Before any of them could make a move, armed men appeared from the side of the road.

"Get out of the car," a tall, dark-haired man ordered as he slowly walked towards them. He was unarmed; clearly, he thought his men had enough weapons to control the situation that he didn't need any.

Reluctantly, Jack, Tony, and Dark exited the vehicle, holding their hands up to show they were unarmed. They knew the drill well enough not to give them any excuse to open fire on them.

The leader of the group walked up to them, giving them the once-over.

"You will come with us. No sudden moves, or my men will open fire. My orders are to bring you to my boss, they do not stipulate in what condition," he said confidently.

Jack did a quick check on how many men and their positioning.

After a quick head count, he deduced there were two at the rear of the convoy, two facing them and the leader, who seemed to be unarmed.

He passed Dark a quick glance and saw that he, too, had been doing the same thing. Without needing to say anything, they both knew what to do, they just had to synchronize.

He flashed Dark a quick series of hand signals to let him know what he intended and when.

The armed men stepped forward to enforce the orders given by their leader. Jack felt a gun barrel prod him in the back to urge him to move.

A glance at Dark told him the time to move was now.

Spinning around, he knocked the barrel of the rifle away from him as he punched the shooter in the face. Before the man could react, he had torn the rifle away from him and turned it on him. A quick three-shot burst ended his threat along with his life as the bullets stitched a path across his chest, sending him sprawling back into the dirt.

He spun to face Dark, who had done the same, smashing the butt of the AK into the face of his attacker before sending him on his way with a burst from the rifle. They both turned to face the others but were amazed to see Tony had the leader by the throat, threatening to kill him if the other two didn't drop their guns.

While they were deciding what to do, Jack dispatched them both with a burst from his AK.

As Tony faced him, he just said, "We don't have the time to fuck around."

Dark was at his side, grabbing the leader and aiming his AK at his face.

"Jack's right, they'll be expecting us, so we need to know where and how many."

Once Jack had rounded up all the other weapons from the dead men, he came to stand with the others.

"Right, we have a Glock each and one over and four AKs, so at least we have the weapons we wanted."

"What about your friend over there?" Dark asked, indicating Papandrou who was standing by his car watching them, his eyes wide. In all the excitement, they had forgotten about him.

Jack put his hand on Tony's arm to stop him from storming off.

"He gave us up, he's no friend of mine," he said through gritted teeth. He yanked his arm free and strode over to him.

"Should we stop him?" Dark asked, unsure of what to do.

"Tony's right, he gave us up just as we suspected. He deserves what's coming to him."

"Okay then, that just leaves you," Dark said, returning his attention to the leader of the attackers. "Where were you taking us?"

The leader's confidence had all but left him. Jack could see in his posture and by the terror in his eyes that he was afraid, but he also knew they needed him for information, for now at least.

Tony walked up to the defiant Papandrou, holding the Glock Jack handed to him.

"Are you going to kill me too?" the Greek asked.

"You gave us up, maybe I should. You certainly deserve it."

"And what do you deserve, Tony, for killing my family?"

"I didn't kill them, you must know that."

"But you did nothing to prevent it, and by your actions, sending those men here, you set in motion the events that led to their death. If you had left well alone, none of this would have happened."

"You'd like to think so."

"What does that mean?"

"Maria called me and asked for my help. If I had said no, she would have found someone else. She wanted out from under the heel of whoever was extorting her family."

"Maybe, but maybe not."

"I tried to help, damnit."

"And you failed."

"This is going nowhere. You'd better leave."

"I'm a dead man when they find out I failed them."

"They won't find out, so don't worry."

"How can you be so sure?"

"Because we're going to kill them all."

Tony turned around and walked off, his face stern, as he knew he would never see his friend again.

"Right, you're going to tell me what I want to know now, or you will die. It's as simple as that," Jack told the leader.

"You won't kill me, you need information. All I have

to do is hold out until they know we're not coming, and they'll send someone else. Go ahead, do your worst, you don't frighten me," he replied with a snarl.

"I said I would kill you, I didn't say it would be quick or painless, and I didn't say it would be today," Jack said with a stony expression.

"You think I'm a fool? I know you need information now and fast. You don't have time to prolong this," the leader countered as his confidence grew.

Dark rifled through their captive's pockets until he found what he was looking for. He tossed the phone to Jack.

"This is all we need. Everything we need will be on there, so we don't need him anymore," he said calmly and coldly.

"He's right. Once we access that, you don't need to keep him alive," Tony agreed as he walked back to them.

Jack saw fear blossom in the man's eyes for the first time. He thrust his hands into the pockets of his trousers.

"It's got a fingerprint scanner on it," Jack said recognizing the involuntary move on his part.

"He doesn't need to be alive for us to use that, all we need is a finger," Tony said.

Before Jack could respond, Tony put the Glock to the side of the leader's head and pulled the trigger. The man's skull distorted as the bullet traveled through, sending a stream of red gore across the ground before he dropped like a stone.

Jack stared at Tony, "You said it yourself, we're running out of time."

"I just hope Deakin can get something off this phone then, seeing as how you just killed our last lead," Jack said as he reached for his phone to make the call.

CHAPTER FORTY-FIVE

Robert Deakin was getting worried. It had been almost a full day since he'd heard from them.

He was sure someone from MI6 was going to come back to check up on him any time now. He kept looking over his shoulder as he came back to work. The security guards placed at the entrance, presumably by Bennett, had allowed him to come back into the building, even though much of it was still under lockdown because of the damage. He assumed it was because he still had work to do in compiling the files Bennett wanted him to send to MI6. Whatever the reason, it didn't help ease his anxiety over the whole situation.

He wasn't a field agent, and even though he wasn't actually in the field, it felt like he was on a mission with the guys. He felt he should be excited to be included; instead, he was terrified.

What would happen if they caught him communicating with them after they had been ordered to stand down? Was this something he could go to prison for?

Was this treason, and if so, didn't they still hang people for that?

He had to get himself under control; thoughts like these were not good and diverted him away from what he should be doing. Nevertheless, he almost jumped out of his skin when his phone rang.

"Jack, where the hell are you? Is Tony there? What about the Commander? What's going on? Why haven't you called sooner?" he blurted out all his frustrations. Jack's calm voice did nothing to soothe his anxiety.

"Slow down, Robert, we're all here, and we're fine. I just need you to extract as much data as you can from this phone. I'm sending you the number now," Jack said.

Robert looked at the screen, and sure enough, a number appeared as a text message.

"I'll do what I can," he replied.

"Do it now, Robert, it's important, and I need it *now*."

"Jeez, Jack, nothing is ever easy with you, is it?"

"You wouldn't like it if it was. I know you, Robert. You thrive on a challenge."

"Okay, just give me a sec."

"I'll hold the line," Jack told him.

Robert went to his station and sat down to enter the phone number into the computer. He placed his phone down by the side of the keyboard and put it on speaker. His fingers danced across the keys almost as if they had a mind of their own as he connected to the device. In a few short moments, he had downloaded everything possible from the phone.

"I'm sending a file to all your phones with everything I got from it," he said, pressing the 'send' key with a flourish.

"Thanks, Robert, as usual, you're a lifesaver," Jack said and closed the connection.

Jack turned to Tony, "I've got it."

The other two looked at their phones as the data came through to them all simultaneously.

"Wow, he works fast," Dark commented.

"Deakin is the best at what he does," Tony agreed.

"Okay, it's not a lot, but it tells us what we're dealing with here," Jack said as he scrolled through the file.

"That's a heady mix, the Cartels aligning with the Mafia to control the drug trade coming through this area and beyond," Tony observed as he, too, read the file.

"Seems like they neglected the extortion racket somewhat in favor of this new enterprise, good news for the residents, I suppose," Dark added.

"This is your call, Tony, how do we play this?" Jack asked.

Tony looked up from his phone.

"I have an idea, we play to our strengths."

CHAPTER FORTY-SIX

Vaughn was a patient man, but this was becoming almost too difficult to maintain, not because he was getting bored or anything like that, it was simply because he was beginning to attract attention to himself, and in his line of work, that was a complete disaster.

He got up to pay the bill when he saw the three men he'd been asked to watch head towards the jetty.

I must be slipping; I never saw them arrive.

He sat back down and waved the waiter over. Things were about to heat up, so he ordered another coffee, took out his phone, and pretended to check a few things out on it. He couldn't leave now, not when things were finally about to get interesting.

As he watched the trio head towards the small motor launch that had brought a group of men from the yacht to shore, he realized how much fun he was having. His thoughts of retiring here suddenly didn't seem so important anymore. He drank his coffee and then paid the bill, leaving a generous tip. He got in his car, an old Nissan, then drove away from the tavern and up onto the ridge that overlooked the bay. He would have a better vantage point for what he needed to do from there, and he was away from any prying eyes.

As he parked, he got out, went to the rear of the car, took out a long slim case, and then returned to his car. He opened the case and started to assemble the rifle it had contained.

It didn't take long before he could look through the scope at what was happening on board the yacht.

———

Tony walked up to the motor launch as bold as brass.

"I want to go over to that yacht, and you're going to take me," he commanded the lone sailor sitting on the jetty with his feet up against one of the poles that sat up a few feet from the jetty decking.

He looked Tony up and down, then glanced at the other two men standing at his shoulder. With a dismissive wave of his hand, he said, "Fuck off."

He was in the act of lighting another cigarette from the lit end of the one he was already smoking when Tony hoisted him to his feet, both hands grabbing the collar of his dirty shirt.

"I don't think you understand me. I really want to go visit that yacht," Tony said, holding the man close to his face so he could stare into his eyes. The sailor's head was pushed up slightly as Tony placed the tip of his Glock under his chin to push his point home.

The sailor's eyes went wide as he stared death in the face and tried to nod his head. The Glock prevented it from happening, but Tony knew he had him.

"O...okay, I'll take you," he stammered.

Tony released him and pushed him towards the motor

launch, where he stumbled aboard. Tony kept the Glock on him just to let him know there was no escape as he followed him on board.

Jack and Dark both joined them on deck after casting off for the sailor.

They motored out on the sea, heading towards the yacht. Tony kept his Glock aimed at the sailor just in case he tried something stupid like trying to warn them.

It didn't take them long to reach their destination, and Tony stepped up to stand behind the sailor.

"This is where I take over," Tony said.

The sailor looked over his shoulder, his eyes wide upon hearing those words. He glanced into the boat behind Tony, and a confused expression took over.

Tony hit him with the butt of his Glock at the base of his skull, and his lights went out before he could ask any questions. Tony stepped over the fallen sailor and took over the controls.

He continued steering the boat up to the yacht and slowed the engine, allowing it to coast up to it.

Jack quickly tied up the boat beneath the ladder at the rear of the yacht so they could climb aboard. Tony went first and was greeted at the top by two men holding automatic weapons aimed at him.

"Afternoon, gentlemen, thought we'd pop over for a visit, you know, check out the views and whatnot," he said as he calmly stepped onto the deck.

"Who the fuck are you people?" asked one of the men as he watched Jack join Tony on the deck.

With the deckhand's attention diverted by the arrival of the second intruder, Tony saw his chance to act.

"Your worst nightmare," he said, reaching for the Glock in his waistband at the small of his back. He whipped out the pistol and shot the nearest gunman in the face, then shot the other one before Jack could react.

"*Your worst nightmare?* Is that the best you could come up with?" Jack asked, pulling out his own Glock.

"I've always wanted to say that," Tony said with a shrug.

"Well, next time, a little warning first before you go ahead and do something this crazy would be appreciated, thank you."

"Jack."

"What?"

"I think it's time to get a little crazy," Tony said, indicating for him to go down the starboard side whilst he took the port side.

Time to go to work.

"How long before the plane arrives back here?" Andrei asked.

Sergei looked at the time on his laptop and said, "It's due back anytime now."

Andrei heard the shots and was galvanized into motion. He was out of his seat in a flash and reaching for his pistol, making Sergei jump out of his skin.

He'd seen the approach of the motor launch and had assumed it was his men returning with the three agents. The gunshots told him something different.

He had sent enough men to handle three agents, but knowing their capabilities from recent activities, maybe he should have sent more. Hindsight, as they say, is twenty-twenty vision, so it was best to not overthink it and just move on. Deal with the situation as it presented itself now and handle it.

He was still on the foredeck, beneath the awning shielding him from the midday sun, he stood still listening for any signs of movement. The few guards he had left on board had gone to greet the motor launch, leaving him, Sergei, and two others on board.

"Sergei, go grab a weapon. I think we have company," he said, warning the smaller man.

He saw him take a pistol from the back of his waistband and jack the slide after placing his beloved laptop carefully on the deck.

The two of them carefully moved to greet the intruders. Andrei knew that his friend wouldn't let him down. Yes, he was a geek, a computer nerd, but he was also a soldier. They had both been members of the Spetsnaz, the Russian elite Special Forces, so he was adept at close-quarter combat and had killed in battle before. He knew he could rely on him.

Andrei went to the port side, leaving the starboard side to his friend.

It could only be those SI6 agents trying to finish this, he thought. They had one thing right, it would end here, but not like they had planned.

CHAPTER FORTY-SEVEN

Tony could hear someone approaching down his side of the yacht. He didn't care who it was, but he hoped it would be Andrei. He had a score to settle with him for the death of his long-time friend and boss, Bainbridge.

Pressing his back against the hull, he slowed his pace. Holding his Glock against his chest, he calmed his breathing. He knew Andrei was in prime fitness whereas, although he was fit for his age, he was nowhere near combat fit. He had spent too many years sitting behind a desk to count as active service, but he was not about to allow that to intimidate him. He had experience on his side, something the younger man hadn't had the time in his shorter career to accumulate. It would have to be enough.

Petrov had to pay, and he was determined to make him.

———

Andrei stepped out onto the deck. He reached up and placed a hand on the hull, then placed one foot on the railing to push his bulk up off the deck.

Grabbing hold of the roof of the bridge, he pushed off the railing and used all the strength in his broad upper body to pull himself up. It had taken but a few seconds to gain this vantage point. From his elevated platform, he could see the Colonel coming down the side of the yacht, looking, no doubt, for him.

The Colonel and Bainbridge had been close friends for years, even back to the time he had commanded the hit on Bainbridge to prevent him from taking over SI6. He hadn't counted on the two men's stubbornness preventing his men from completing their task, something that had bothered him to this day. When the mission came up to strike at them once more, he jumped at the chance to erase the one black mark in his career. The addition of the death of his brother only added fuel to his anger.

He would have done this for free, instead, the Hierarchy deemed it necessary to compensate him for his loss, something he was not about to rebuke.

So far, he had completed one part of his mission, Bainbridge was dead, and SI6 crippled. Now he was about to finish with the rest of them.

Keeping his body low against the roof of the bridge, he waited for Armstrong to come a few steps closer before he would pounce.

Jack crept along the deck, knowing there were more guards somewhere, plus the two Russians they had come to kill.

This was not a capture and detain op, this was a pure and simple termination.

If this was to be their last mission for SI6, he wanted it to count for something. Petrov had a lot to answer for, as did the Hierarchy, but that was a mission for another time.

This...here...was all he had time to think about. What happened in the next few moments would decide their futures, and he could afford no slip-ups.

Tony edged along the deck, keeping his back to the bridge's hull. He had his breathing under control and was watchful of his surroundings.

The remaining two guards had come from below, obviously summoned by the sound of gunfire.

They quickly checked the situation and then separated at the aft deck, each going after one of the intruders.

Tony heard the deck hand come around the side of the yacht just before a hailstorm of bullets slammed into the hull plating of the bridge.

Chunks of the fiberglass hull were sent scattering into the air from the bullet strikes, showering him with the fine dust. Calmly he turned and fired at the panicked shooter, who quickly dived behind the flybridge for cover.

Tony knew having his attention diverted like that could be deadly, and when he turned back to face the prow, a heavy weight landed on his shoulders, knocking him to the deck.

He went flying onto the hard polished deck, all the breath knocked out of him from the impact.

Trying to regain his feet, he was restricted by the weight still applied to his top half.

He was confused a little by the suddenness of the action until he realized Andrei, or someone, had maneuvered around him and attacked from above.

"Surprise, surprise," Andrei gloated as he pressed down on him from above.

Tony's right hand still had hold of the Glock, but Andrei grabbed his wrist and began to slam it against the deck.

Pain lanced through his wrist, and he was forced to let go of his only weapon and watch it skip across the deck to fly out through an opening and into the sea.

He felt the weight lifted from him Obviously, Andrei thought he could handle him in close-quarter combat, unarmed.

Tony scrambled to his knees, then sprang at Andrei, tackling him around the waist, hoping to slam him against the bulkhead. Instead, he felt like he had shoulder charged a tree. His shoulder exploded in pain as he collided with the Russian's midsection.

What is this guy made of?

Tony felt hands grip his arms and rip them free, and he was suddenly pushed away from his target. He threw a swift right cross at the smug face in front of him, which caught the Russian off guard momentarily. Tony reckoned he didn't expect an old guy like him to move that fast.

The punch knocked Andrei's head around, splitting his lip. He turned back to look at him, and Tony saw pure fury in those eyes.

Andrei rained a flurry of incredibly fast punches at Tony's head. He managed to block most of them on his arms or shoulders, but a few got through, either under his blocks to land on his ribs or over them to bounce off the top of his head. After a while, he was reeling from the onslaught, and he began to think it would never stop.

He lashed out in desperation with a low kick aimed anywhere near the Russian's legs but missed completely, throwing himself off balance for a second. Just for a moment, his head was unprotected as he tried to regain his balance, but that was all Andrei needed.

A right hand connected with his jaw, snapping his head around and sending him to his knees.

Stars danced in front of his eyes as he almost lost consciousness. He felt powerful hands lift him off the deck and force him over to the railing. As he was slammed into the metal poles that ran around the deck, he felt his back groan against the sudden battering. Pain from the impact made him grimace, and he felt the hands change their grip and find his throat.

His feet were lifted off the deck as the Russian was trying to choke him and toss him overboard at the same time. Either meant certain death.

The pressure on his throat meant he couldn't breathe. He tried to pry the fingers free to get some air into his already starving lungs, but his waning strength couldn't find any purchase.

His vision began to fade, and he knew he was losing this fight.

Jack saw the other deckhand come running towards him, rifle ready to fire.

One quickly aimed and fired shot from his Glock soon changed all that, and the deckhand went tumbling over his own feet as he dived for cover.

Another shot rang out, and he hoped it was Tony

firing and not getting shot. He couldn't worry about that at the moment; he had other things to worry about.

Where was the other Russian?

His question was soon answered as Sergei suddenly appeared in front of him, aiming a pistol at his head.

Reacting instinctively, Jack swung his own pistol up and fired. He only heard the one gunshot, but he saw the muzzle flash of the pistol aimed straight at him.

He felt a sudden searing pain in his ears as the gunshot, so close to his head, almost deafened him. He had managed to move his head to the side just in time to prevent a bullet from smacking him in the center of his forehead.

Not taking his eyes off his opponent, he saw the Russian stumble back as a red splash appeared on his chest just below his collarbone. As the blond man stumbled back a step or two, the red smear began to spread as blood from his wound oozed through onto his shirt. The pain and shock in the young man's eyes turned to disbelief as he realized he was about to die.

Jack fired once more to make certain. This time, the bullet took off the top of Sergei's head, sending him crashing to the deck in a convulsive mess.

Breathing a little easier, Jack turned to look through the bridge window to the other side of the yacht. He saw Tony being manhandled by the larger of the two Russians. By the look of his friend, he knew he didn't have long before Andrei got the better of him and hauled him overboard. He also knew there was nothing he could do. He wouldn't reach him in time to help. All he could do was watch as his friend was going to die.

CHAPTER FORTY-EIGHT

Commander Dark exploded from the water holding his Glock in his right hand. His swim from the motor launch and to the opposite side of the yacht had taken longer than he'd hoped.

He had been the best candidate for this type of mission as he was a member of the SBS and had special training in underwater tactics.

A ladder was attached to the outside hull of the yacht, which he quickly grabbed onto, hauling himself free of the water's grip.

Above him, he saw Tony being held in a death grip by Andrei Petrov. He looked about to pass out from the chokehold he had around his throat. After that, there was no doubt the Russian would toss him overboard.

Something else alerted him to another danger. The remaining two deckhands were creeping up on the fight with their rifles leveled and ready to fire. If Andrei didn't finish Tony off, these two surely would.

Taking a quick aim and steadying himself on the ladder, Dark fired the Glock.

Vaughn had the yacht in his sights, and he watched with avid interest.

These guys are good.

He saw Dark climb out of the water on the side of the yacht, which diverted his attention from one particular incident he had been keeping tabs on, the fight between Andrei and Colonel Armstrong.

He was rooting for the Colonel; he knew of his career and knew what he was capable of, but watching this fight, it quickly became obvious that too many years of sitting behind a desk had taken a toll on his fitness. He was in danger of losing this fight, something he alone could prevent, but it had to look like an accident.

He watched as Commander Dark took aim at the approaching deckhands, then took a deep breath as he took aim.

He waited for Dark to fire so his own shot would blend in with that one.

Dark fired at the nearest deckhand, sending him crashing against the bulkhead, then fired again at the other one. Before he even knew where the bullet was coming from, he had been hit and was on the deck.

As he changed his aim to Andrei, he noticed he wasn't there.

The bullet creased Andrei's shoulder, sending a splash of blood across his face from the grazing impact. He staggered back, releasing his hold on Tony, who slumped to the deck, gasping for breath.

Where the fuck had that shot come from?

The shock of the bullet hitting him sent him into a frenzy of rage. He looked out towards the shore, and he could swear he saw the sun glint off a reflective surface up on the ridge.

Was that where the shot had been fired from? If so, they had backup from a sniper, which meant if he remained on board, he was a dead man. He had to get away.

Panic swarmed over him like a living thing, and he turned and ran to the aft section of the yacht, stepping over the dead bodies of the remaining two deckhands.

He had to get away. He could almost feel the sniper bearing down on him, the back of his head in the center of his crosshairs, just waiting to pull the trigger and send him to oblivion.

He reached the rear railing of the yacht close to where the motor launch was tied up and climbed over onto the ladder to climb down.

With Andrei out of the way, Dark carefully continued to climb up to the deck.

Dark's attention was diverted then by the sound of a seaplane flying overhead, circling as it prepared to land.

Hurriedly, he climbed the ladder, keeping one eye trained on the top of the railing should the Russian show his head again.

The sound of the seaplane got louder as it came in to land on the water close to the yacht.

The moment he reached the top of the ladder, he saw

Andrei hightailing it for the aft section of the yacht, where the motor launch was tied up.

Vaulting over the railing, he knelt beside Tony to check his vitals.

"I'm okay," Tony said breathlessly, "get after him."

Dark got to his feet and did as ordered.

Jack saw the large Russian almost ready to throw Tony overboard, then suddenly jump back as blood spurted from the top of his shoulder. The sound of two gunshots registered on his hearing then, but he could have sworn there was a third hidden amongst the rapid, almost double tap, smothered by the sound of the seaplane arriving, and he knew what had happened, Dark had arrived in time.

He watched as Andrei dropped Tony, who crumpled to the deck. He'd never seen the Colonel beaten like that, but no one was invincible.

Andrei turned and ran from sight. He couldn't see what was happening until he saw Dark climb over the railing.

He glanced at the aft of the yacht, his attention drawn there by the sound of the seaplane coming in to land, and he saw Andrei hurl himself over the railing where they had tied up the motor launch.

"Shit, fuck!!" he snarled, as he knew what was about to happen.

Running over to the railing, he hoped to catch Andrei, but he was too late, the Russian had disappeared. Andrei had already untied the launch and was heading out to the seaplane.

He spotted the trailing rope used to tie it up still

close by in the water. Without thinking, he vaulted the railing, landing on the lip on the other side, then shoving his Glock in the waistband of his chinos, he dived headlong into the water.

As his head breached the surface, he saw the rope disappearing under the water as the motor launch picked up speed. Taking a deep breath, he went under, looking for the rope. It was there, beginning to come up once more as the launch's progression through the water began to drag it after it.

He thrust himself through the water, his arms making powerful strokes to catch it. He was within reach, but a sudden lurch flicked it free. Desperation began to take roost, and he stroked through the water like an Olympic swimmer in the final race of their career wanting to go out on a high until he caught it.

His right hand closed around it, and he felt his shoulder socket almost pop from the drag through the water. He managed to get his other hand on it to get a firmer grip, and he was pulled through the water.

He had to kick his legs beneath him to angle his progression at an upward angle to enable him to breach the surface once more. His lungs were aching from holding his breath. He desperately wanted to breathe in but knew if he did that, he would just take in water and drown.

Stars began to dance before his eyes, and he kicked even harder. He had to reach the surface in the next few seconds, or all would be lost.

Just when his grip was beginning to slacken through his lack of air, he felt his head break free into the open air. He quickly filled his lungs, just in case he was dragged under again.

He was pulled along just on the edge of the water,

dipping below the surface on occasion, but by the time he had his bearings, he was okay to pull himself along the rope to close the gap.

Hand over agonizing hand, he pulled against the weight and force of the water until he thought his shoulder sockets would pop. Then, as the launch slowed as it neared the seaplane, he had the chance to pull himself along faster, gaining momentum with every handful of rope he grabbed.

The launch slowed and came to a complete stop. Jack looked up and saw Andrei jump from it to the pontoon of the seaplane.

He had very little time left now to make his move. Stroking like his life depended upon it, he surged forward through the water just in time to see the large Russian slam the door shut.

CHAPTER FORTY-NINE

Andrei was nursing a sore shoulder when he bounded from the motor launch onto the pontoon of the seaplane.

Where had that shot come from? Had they backup he hadn't seen or thought of? Someone was definitely looking out for them; that's why he had to get away.

Wrenching the door of the aircraft open, he was greeted with the frightened stare of the pilot. The big Russian was the last person he had expected to see, and Andrei used it to his advantage.

Slamming the door behind him, he shouted, "Do not turn off those engines."

He bunched his shoulders as he stepped into the forward cabin and grabbed the pilot by the scruff of his jacket, yanking him from his seat. A swift punch to the temple knocked all the fight from him, and he dragged him over to the door.

"This is where you get off," he said as he opened the door. Instead of seeing only the waters of the Aegean, something else greeted him, something, someone he did not expect.

"You!"

Jack pulled himself onto the pontoon, his arms beginning to feel like jelly from his exertions.

He knew he had to get inside the plane before it took off or run the risk of falling off. Failure, this close to his objective, was not an option.

Gathering his last reserves of strength, he pulled himself fully onto the pontoon and steadied himself as he reached for the door when it suddenly opened.

The startled look on Andrei's face changed as he pushed the pilot through the opening right at him.

The two of them collided, almost knocking him back into the sea. As he struggled to free himself from the desperate clutches of the flailing pilot, he saw the door slam once more.

He knew the plane would start to move in seconds, and his chances of getting on board were dwindling rapidly.

The plane began to move as he finally fended off the grabbing hands of the pilot, as he eventually fell into the sea. Almost losing his balance, Jack grabbed onto the strut that held the wing onto the fuselage. Once he'd regained his balance, he reached for the door.

The speed of the plane increased, and he felt the wind buffeting him as it tried to tear him free. Water splashed him as the plane bounced on the water, trying to gain the momentum needed to lift off.

The wind speed worked against him as he opened the door and had to force it against the streamlining effect of the wind. It was like he was trying to push the door open against a heavy wind.

The door was almost torn from his grasp and would have slammed shut if not for him placing his shoulder against it to prevent that from happening. With a huge effort, he finally got it open enough for him to climb through before the wind slammed it closed behind him.

He slumped down, almost at the point of exhaustion, just long enough to regain his breath.

Andrei glanced over his shoulder from the pilot's seat as he entered the plane. His intention was plain from the look of fury in his eyes.

Jack placed his feet beneath him and launched himself at the pilot. He wrapped an arm around the Russian's thick neck and pulled tight. He grabbed the crook of his other arm's elbow with the hand of the arm around Andrei's neck and placed that hand on the back of Andrei's head, effectively locking the chokehold in firmly.

As he pulled his arm across Andrei's throat and levered that with the hand on the back of the Russian's head, he could apply an enormous pressure on the throat, pinching the carotid artery. In a few seconds, Andrei would realize air was not getting to his brain, his vision would start to star, then, as his brain was starved of air, he would black out. If the hold was held thirty seconds more, he would die.

Jack had every intention of holding the chokehold on for as long as possible, until the inevitable happened.

At least, that was the plan.

Jack leaned forward to apply even more pressure on the hold, but he never expected the retaliation, at least not in the confines of the pilot's cabin.

As Jack's head came forward, Andrei brought his left knee up sharply to smack it against Jack's face.

Jack saw it coming just in time to turn his head sideways just enough to take the blow on his cheek rather than full in the face. Even so, the pain from the blow was enough for him to see stars and release the hold.

He staggered back, his hands automatically coming up to cover his face.

Jack fell back as Andrei pulled back on the controls and boosted the power. The seaplane's nose pointed towards the sky as it took to the air. The incline got steeper as the speed increased, and Jack found himself tumbling backward. He grabbed hold of the inside of the plane to stop himself from falling into the tail section.

Hand over hand, he fought against the incline to get back to the front of the plane. By the time he reached the door, Andrei was leveling the seaplane out.

He saw him turn a switch and mess with something else on the myriad of dials and switches on the control panel before turning back towards him.

He must've activated the autopilot.

Jack greeted him with a grimace of pure hatred as the Russian got out of the pilot's seat to come and meet him. This was a meeting Jack had been looking forward to but one that could only have one outcome.

Only one of them would get out of there alive.

Vaughn watched Jack swim out to the seaplane and kept his sights fixed on the action just in case he needed to help out again.

He had been lucky so far, no one seemed to be asking questions, and that's how he wanted it to remain.

He kept watch as Jack pulled himself onto the pontoon after the large Russian, and he wondered by the look of him if he'd manage to pull this off on his own.

Once he got on board the plane, *if* he got on board, then there was nothing he could do to help other than bring the plane down, and that would be more than a little tricky. In fact, it would be nigh on impossible to accomplish without giving himself away.

He just had to hope these agents were as good as Bennett seemed to think they were.

CHAPTER FIFTY

The two of them collided just aft of the pilot's cabin, hands grabbing at anything to gain an advantage.

Jack knocked the Russian's hands off his collar before they could get a better grip, then punched him full in the face.

The punch did little other than to turn his head away and increase the man's fury. When he looked at him once more, Jack could've sworn that his eyes glowed red with anger.

Jack swung another punch, but it was blocked by Andrei's forearm, who then countered with a punch of his own.

Jack's head was rocked back by the powerful blow, and he almost lost his footing. Before he knew what was happening, a torrent of punches rained down on him, and he had to cover up to save himself from serious damage.

Ducking low, he forced himself off the fuselage where Andrei had him pinned, slamming his shoulder into the midsection of the Russian. A satisfying grunt from the big man as he rammed him against the other side of the craft told him he could be hurt.

Letting go of his attacker's waist, he delivered an uppercut to his chin, which rocked Andrei's head back, bouncing it off the fuselage behind. Jack followed up with a left hook to the ribs, then a right cross to the side of his head, sending him to the deck, blood streaming from his mouth.

Andrei came up from the floor fast, crashing into Jack, startling him with the intensity and speed. They both collided with the opposite side of the craft, with Jack taking the full force of the impact. His breath exploded from him, followed quickly by a wave of pain centered on his back area.

Andrei started throwing punches in a frenzy at him, and he felt his strength waning from the onslaught.

Thoughts of his dead family invaded his mind, then he realized if he didn't do something fast, he would be joining them in the next few moments.

Part of him wanted that, for all this heartache to end, for the pain to subside, and for him not to care what happened to the world for a change. He began to ask why was it always left up to the likes of him to protect innocents when he couldn't even protect those he loved most in the world?

Deep down, he knew the answer, and he remembered what Major Bacon had told him when he was brought back into SI6. He had told him that he was a soldier and they handled matters that the general public would rather not sully their hands on. This was one of those matters.

As Andrei drew his arm up to deliver a huge strike from above, Jack saw his chance.

He struck a straight finger jab into the unprotected

throat of his attacker. Andrei's eyes went wide as his throat closed and he began to choke.

Jack drew his knees up to his chest and lashed out with both feet, smacking them into Andrei's chest and sending him sprawling into the opposite wall.

Jack was on him then, punching him repeatedly in the face, opening cut after cut as he rained down his fury and frustration on him, battering his face to a pulp. Blood smeared his knuckles and he stepped back to look down on the defeated form of his attacker.

He grabbed him by the collar and dragged him to his feet. By this time, he was barely awake and could hardly breathe. Without a word, Jack opened the door and tossed the Russian out of the plane, closing the door and that chapter of his life.

He staggered back to the pilot's cabin and dropped into the seat. A quick check of the instruments told him all he needed to know. Switching off the autopilot, he grabbed hold of the controls and took manual control.

Touching his ear bud, he said, "Tony, I'm bringing the plane back. Andrei is dead, it's over."

The moment Vaughn saw Andrei pushed from the plane, he knew his job was over.

Taking a deep, relaxing breath, he started to put away his rifle.

Now that was over, he could get back to enjoying himself again.

CHAPTER FIFTY-ONE

The three of them returned to Fairfax later that night and went straight to SI6 HQ, where Deakin was still waiting for them.

"It's about time you got back. I had no idea what I'd have told Bennett if he'd called," the small IT expert said as he saw them enter.

"Nice to see you too, Robert," Jack said with a raised eyebrow.

Before any of them could say anything else, Tony's phone rang.

The ID screen told him the number was 'Private', but he suspected he knew who was calling.

"Hello, Deputy Director. What can I do for you?" he said, holding his phone to his ear.

"I hope you had a pleasant time on Crete and that you're all well rested on your flight home?" Bennett said, completely unperturbed that Tony knew it was him calling.

"Thank you, and I wouldn't say well rested, but we are good, thanks."

"I also trust you completed your mission satisfactorily?"

Tony glanced at the others, his eyes going wide. Not letting any of the surprise he was feeling filter through to his voice, he said, "If by that you're asking if Petrov is dead, then the answer is a categoric yes."

"Then congratulations are in order from me. Come straight here for your debrief," Bennett said, ending the call before Tony could object.

"He wants us there pronto for a debrief," he said, looking up at them all.

Jack said, "Well, might as well get it over with then so we can move on with our lives."

"You too, Robert. Let's see what he has in store for you, too, shall we?" Tony told the IT expert.

———

The staff car took them all to MI6, where they were escorted to Bennett's office. Four chairs were already in place in front of his impressive desk for when they arrived.

"Glad you could make it. Please take a seat, everyone. I'll try to get through this as fast as I can so you can all away to your beds."

They all sat and waited for the inevitable roasting they knew was coming their way for disobeying a direct order.

"Now, the official debrief will be short and sweet and will take place in a few days. I more or less know what went on over there. All I need from you all are some corroborating details."

Tony leaned forward, "So what is the meaning of this meeting then?" he asked pointedly.

"To inform you of your positions now that SI6 has been disbanded. I told you before you left that due to the severity and public nature of the recent attacks, we had to place the blame somewhere, and where better than on an organization that has since paid the price and been punished by being disbanded?

"Gentlemen, we live in a transparent world where everything is either on YouTube or on the Internet in some form or other. There is no place left in the world for shadowy groups and units like SI6. That is the official opinion of our government, and I am here to issue you all with your P45s, so to speak."

The four men exchanged glances, none of them any clearer as to what the future held for them. All they knew was they were sacked, but what exactly did that mean?

"I'm not sure if I'm hearing you right. Are you saying we're fired?" he asked.

"That is exactly what I'm saying, fired from SI6. You will, of course, continue to be employed by me."

"Now we're getting to it," Jack said with a smile.

"Jack, you will be put on indefinite leave on emotional grounds. You can have the time you need to deal with your loss. Go grieve properly, and when you're ready to come back, I'm sure we can find something for you to do."

"And if I decide I don't want to come back?"

Bennett looked him straight in the eye and said, "That is entirely up to you. If you choose not to return though, you do realize you'll still be bound by the Official Secrets Act?"

Jack nodded. "I can live with that."

"Commander Dark, I understand you were loaned out to SI6 from your previous commander in the SBS, is that correct?"

Dark cleared his throat before answering in the affirmative.

"Well, in your case, it's a simple RTU then. I'm sure your commander will be more than happy to let you have command of 'C' Squadron once more. Now, on to you, Mister Deakin. I understand you ran the R&D section of SI6. MI6 can always use someone of your expertise, you will be a valuable asset here, I'm sure."

Tony looked at Bennett, waiting for his turn.

Bennett looked across his desk at the four of them. "Well, I think that covers just about everything. The debrief will begin in a day or two, someone will be in touch. Until then, you can all take a few days to recover from your ordeal, all except you, Colonel. I'd like a private word with you alone."

They all knew they had been dismissed, so Jack, Dark, and Deakin got up to leave.

When they had left, Tony asked, "What's this about, sir?"

"SI6 may be dead in the water Colonel, but it's been pointed out to me recently that the work your little group did was invaluable. To be perfectly honest with you, I was more than a little jealous of the results you got, but that has nothing to do with my decision here today. In fact, I have a proposition for you."

"I'm listening."

"I want you to head up a small unit to handle only the most extreme of cases. Cases not even we are sanctioned to handle. You would be answerable only to me personally, and I, in turn, to the Prime Minister. It would be a unit of only a few, as few as possible, in fact, and you would have carte blanche on who you picked. It would be a true shadow operation, off the radar with little or no backup."

Tony looked at him, not quite believing what he was hearing. Could a unit like the one he was suggesting actually survive in today's climate of surveillance? Could he run a unit like that? Did he have what was needed to make it work? He had no idea, but he knew he had to try.

Bennett said, "Well, Colonel, are you game?"

The smile he saw returned was all the affirmation Bennett needed.

EPILOGUE

Jack returned home and went into his kitchen to make himself a brew.

He was bone tired, and when he was pouring the boiling water onto the teabag in his favorite mug, he could not stop the jaw-breaking yawn he'd been holding back a moment longer.

He dumped the teabag in the bin after stirring milk into the mug, and he sat at the table staring into space as he thought about this new development.

He had been given time to grieve his lost family, but how was he supposed to do that? When he was in the Army and he lost mates, that was easy, the job made it so. Now though, Bennett had stripped that valuable tool from him. How was he going to cope with nothing to take his mind off the pain?

There was no trick to handling grief, he realized as he sat slowly sipping the hot tea. When he thought back to times when he lost friends, it wasn't the job that helped him heal, it was the job that masked it, gave him something else to think about. He healed in time by just getting through the pain, one day at a time. The pain never really left him; it just got easier to bear.

That was what he was going to have to do now. Just learn to live with the loss.

He would survive, he was certain of that. Even though as he sat there thinking about his wife and daughter, the pain was almost unbearable, he knew he would get through it eventually.

What about the Hierarchy?

They had tried their best to kill him more than once and failed. They were still out there, of that he was just as certain, and they would rise up again to attack the fabric of society, he was certain of that too. What was uncertain was if he would be the one to stand against them.

He would do as Bennett had suggested and give himself some time off to heal. He had been fighting this war for as long as he could remember. He still had plenty of life left in him, even if he thought that at the moment he had nothing to live for, he knew that would change too.

Perhaps it was time to stand down and let someone else take up the mantle. No one could say he hadn't given enough to his country, for he had.

At that moment, he just didn't know, but that would change too.

A LOOK AT BOOK THREE:
An Eye for an Eye

Revenge is indiscriminate, affecting those it seeks…

Jack Cross—still coping with the loss of his family—is visiting with his old partner when a chance meeting with DEA Agent Charlotte Parker sends him on a mission toward catching a ring of corruption that's bigger than meets the eye.

A drug cartel overlord has a plan to wipe out the competition and leave what's left behind for his benefit alone. But the chemist he forcefully hires to work on a new designer drug has other plans and plots his vicious revenge.

Meanwhile, Charlotte is being discredited by her handler, and she and Jack must fight to clear her name…all while preventing a global catastrophe in the name of retribution.

AVAILABLE JUNE 2023

ABOUT THE AUTHOR

Jack Dillon loves to write fast-paced thrillers that have plenty of action. He grew up watching James Bond films, and he read every one of the books he could get his hands on. When other authors started catching his eye—authors such as Clive Cussler, Jack Higgins and, Matthew Reilly—they inspired him to write his own adventures.

So far, Jack has written two series with strong leading characters, the Jack Cross series and the ATLAS Force series. A statistic of the pandemic, he was forced into early retirement. But it wasn't such a bad thing as it gave him the opportunity to write full time, which had been a long-held dream of his.

Living in a beautiful part of the Derbyshire peak district, Jack takes advantage of the wonderful scenery. And when he isn't gazing at it through a window, he can be found finding other ways to procrastinate. Don't worry, though, he still has plenty of ideas that will eventually find their way into a book. At least, that's what he tells himself.

Printed in Great Britain
by Amazon